W/0

Justin picked up her hand and held it between both of his. 'I'm glad you were there.'

Heat flamed its way through Stasy's body at his touch, and she looked down at their hands, then back to his face, seeing his heartfelt thanks reflected in his eyes.

'Well, you know…that's what friends are for,' she stammered, forcing herself to speak. The way he was holding her hand, almost cradling it tenderly, was enough to send her unstable emotions into overdrive. He was looking at her in a way no other man had, and she discovered she liked it very much.

'Is that what we are? Friends?' He rubbed his thumb over the back of her hand, caressing gently.

She was mesmerised by the way he was overpowering her senses. Everything seemed to be going haywire. When Justin looked at her she recognised desire in his eyes, and she wasn't sure how she should react. Her heart-rate was starting to increase, forcing her breathing to follow suit, and she parted her lips, unable to break from his gaze.

BACHELOR DADS
Single Doctor... Single Father!

At work they are skilled medical professionals, but at home, as soon as they walk in the door, these eligible bachelors are on full-time fatherhood duty!

These devoted dads
still find room in their lives for love...

It takes very special women to win the hearts of these dedicated doctors, and a very special kind of caring to make these single fathers full-time husbands!

A WEDDING AT LIMESTONE COAST

BY
LUCY CLARK

MILLS & BOON®
Pure reading pleasure™

First published in Great Britain 2008
Large Print edition 2008
Harlequin Mills & Boon Limited,
Eton House, 18-24 Paradise Road,
Richmond, Surrey TW9 1SR

ISBN: 978 0 263 19990 1

Set in Times Roman 17 on 20 pt.
17-1108-45484

Printed and bound in Great Britain
by Antony Rowe Ltd, Chippenham, Wiltshire

Lucy Clark is actually a husband-and-wife writing team. They enjoy taking holidays with their children, during which they discuss and develop new ideas for their books using the fantastic Australian scenery. They use their daily walks to talk over characterisation and fine details of the wonderful stories they produce, and are avid movie buffs. They live on the edge of a popular wine district in South Australia, with their two children, and enjoy spending family time together at weekends.

Recent titles by the same author:

HER VERY SPECIAL BABY
HIS CHRISTMAS PROPOSAL
THE EMERGENCY DOCTOR'S DAUGHTER
THE SURGEON'S COURAGEOUS BRIDE
IN HIS SPECIAL CARE

To Austin and Melanie—
whose wild imaginations are
starting to match those of their parents!
We love you very much. James 1:19

CHAPTER ONE

THE ringing of the phone on her desk made Anastasia Roberts roll her eyes and she absently picked it up as she signed her name to another set of case notes before closing the file.

'Stasy here,' she said.

'Stasy, we need you.'

'I'll be right there, Christine.' With a sigh, Stasy hung the phone up and looked with loathing at her in-tray. It was piled high with pieces of paper which required her attention and as she'd missed the last board meeting due to an emergency there was now more work for her to slog through than usual. The sooner they hired a head of unit to come and take the administration stuff from her shoulders, the better. She was a doctor who didn't like administration duties. Let someone else have the headaches.

Ignoring the mound of paperwork, she grabbed her stethoscope and headed to A and E. At least here at Limestone Coast Hospital in Mount Gambier, situated near the edge of the Great Australian Bight, the place was small enough that it only took her a minute to walk down the corridor to where there was no sign of the triage sister who'd called her there.

'Where did she go?' Stasy looked around and headed over to treatment room one where, no doubt, the triage sister and Gene, the A and E registrar, would be taking care of whatever emergency had come in to the eighty-bed hospital.

Walking briskly into the treatment area, she headed straight to the sink to wash her hands. 'What have we got?' she asked, not looking round.

'Patient is a Mrs Ienfeld. Sixty-seven-year-old female who fell from a ladder in the front yard of her home,' Christine reported.

'Mrs Ienfeld? Can you hear me?' came a deep, authoritative voice.

That's not Gene. Stasy turned sharply to see a doctor she didn't know standing by the patient. 'Who are you?' She dried her hands and pulled on a pair of gloves, before walking over.

'Nice welcome,' the stranger replied drolly. He turned back to the patient. 'Mrs Ienfeld?' All he received was a murmured but incoherent response.

Stasy picked up the medical torch and checked her patient's pupils. 'Both pupils equal and reacting to light, although a bit sluggish. Sorry. I was just expecting Gene to be in here.'

'He's in cubicle three with another patient,' Christine supplied.

'Right. Thanks.'

The tall, dark and handsome doctor was checking Mrs Ienfeld for injury. 'Right ankle is swollen, bruising starting to occur.' He looked over at Christine. 'You said she fell from a ladder?'

'Yes. She was apparently trying to clean out the gutters. Her husband is disabled.'

'Where's the ambulance report?' Stasy asked.

'Her neighbour brought her in.'

'Moved her and brought her in?' Stasy shook her head.

'Didn't want to bother the ambulance people,' Christine supplied as she secured the patient's neck with a brace.

'They've probably caused more damage in moving her,' the stranger said. 'Possible fracture to right acetabular cup and neck of femur. Cross-type and match.'

'I'm sorry,' Stasy said again, looking over at the new doctor. 'My name is Stasy and I don't want to appear rude, but who are you?'

'I'm Justin,' was all he said as he continued to examine Mrs Ienfeld. Stasy worked with Christine to set up a saline IV, surreptitiously watching him. He certainly seemed competent.

'Justin's the new head of A and E,' Christine said in a whisper.

'The hospital hired someone?' Stasy was too surprised to keep her voice low. She'd been waiting for two years for them to fill the position and in the meantime she'd been left to wade through the paperwork as acting head of department.

'You didn't know?' Justin seemed surprised, then he nodded slowly. 'You're Anastasia Roberts, right?'

'Yes.' How on earth did he know that?

'You missed the last meeting,' he supplied, as though he could read her mind.

'I was unavoidably detained.'

'Attending an emergency.' He nodded as though it was a commonplace occurrence. 'Anyway, I was at the meeting, introducing myself. A memo, as I understand it, was circulated to announce the appointment.'

Stasy nodded her head and closed her eyes for a moment. 'I'm sure there was. I haven't made much progress with reading my mail this past week. It's been a little hectic, especially as Gene was down with a cold for three days.'

'So I understand. Do we have any case notes on Mrs Ienfeld? Has she been to this hospital before? Any allergies?'

'Notes have been ordered. They're being sent up now,' Christine informed him.

'What about the husband?' Stasy asked. 'Or the neighbour who brought her in? Can we get some information from them?'

'The neighbour left to go and take care of the husband,' Christine said with a shrug.

'Mrs Ienfeld?' Stasy called, but the answer was still a mumble. She pressed her fingers to the woman's carotid pulse. 'It's increased. Becoming rapid.'

'Oxygen, stat,' Justin ordered.

'We'll need X-rays once she's stable.'

'Patient has voided,' Christine reported as she finished cutting away Mrs Ienfeld's skirt and draping the lower part of the patient with a warm hospital blanket. Justin was winding the blood-pressure cuff around the patient's arm.

'BP is dropping,' he reported a moment later. 'Mrs Ienfeld?' This time when he called, he received no response. 'Stasy, how's that IV line?'

'All done.' Stasy started the drip which would hopefully boost the woman's BP.

'Notes are here,' one of the nurses announced as she brought them into the room. 'Patient has no known allergies. She and her husband moved to Mount Gambier only six months ago and since then she's only been seen once here and that was for severe headaches. Past medical history shows she's had a left total hip replacement five years ago but apart from that is fit and healthy for her age.'

'Order up a unit of O-negitive,' Justin said as he checked the pulse on the right foot again. 'As far as X-rays go, she'll need right pelvis, right femur, right lower leg and ankle, as well as full spinal column. Is there a CT machine available?'

Stasy ran the end of a reflex hammer up the

base of Mrs Ienfeld's feet, wishing the neighbour hadn't moved the patient but had called
the ambulance instead. 'Motor responses are
medium on the left leg, not good on the right.'
She looked at her new colleague. 'And yes, we
have a fully functional radiology department.
The hospital's not *that* small, Justin.'

'Forgive me,' he replied with a slight nod of
his head. 'I didn't mean to offend—just being
the new boy and putting his foot in it.'

Stasy smiled at his response but concentrated
on her work.

'We'll see how Mrs Ienfeld's radiographs
turn out but she may need a CT scan of her
spine, especially as the neighbour was so sweet
as to shift her.'

Stasy nodded and turned to the nurse who'd
brought in the case notes. 'Get the X-ray
request forms written, contact the ortho-
paedic and general surgical consultants.' She
turned to Christine. 'Draw up morphine,
three milligrams IV.'

'BP is still dropping,' Justin reported. Stasy pressed her fingers to Mrs Ienfeld's carotid pulse.

'Pulse is thready.'

'Pupils are sluggish. Mrs Ienfeld?' he called again, but received no response. Stasy hooked her stethoscope into her ears and listened to the woman's heart and lungs.

'There's a rasping sound.'

'Ready crash cart,' Justin ordered.

Christine pulled the cart over and switched on the machinery. 'Ready.'

'Get an EEG readout.'

Christine nodded and started to set up the EEG machine.

'What's that?' Stasy asked, as the nurse finished cutting away Mrs Ienfeld's clothing. She pointed to a red area on the right side of the woman's chest. Stasy felt it with her fingers and knew a bruise would form there later.

'She must have fallen on something.'

'Respiration is falling, Doctor,' the nurse announced.

'Intubate. She may have a punctured lung.' The oxygen mask was removed and Justin had her intubated with little fuss. Stasy had to admit she was impressed.

'How's the BP?' he asked a moment later.

'No change,' Christine replied.

Stasy was looking at Mrs Ienfeld's right leg. 'The capillary function isn't good. She must have a fracture somewhere else. Possible tib and fib.'

'You think the fracture is obstructing blood flow?'

'I do.'

'Can you straighten it? We need to increase neurovascular function.' Justin moved around the bed, coming to stand beside Stasy. 'Or I can do it if you prefer.'

'It's fine. I've done it before.'

'But these types of things require brute strength.'

'Are you saying I'm not strong enough?' Stasy arched an eyebrow at him as she prepared to do her job. 'Or are you saying that you're a brute?'

As she spoke, she saw his lips twitch a little. Good. It appeared her new boss, for that was what she realised he would be, had a sense of humour. In the next moment she'd straightened the fracture.

'She's going into ventricular fibrilation. Cardiac arrest is imminent,' Christine announced, monitoring the dials. All wires were quickly removed.

'Paddles charged?'

'Ready.'

'Clear!' Justin administered the shock and a moment later Mrs Ienfeld's chest started to rise and fall of its own accord. He handed the paddles to Christine.

'She's in tachy sinus rythym,' Stasy said, before checking the patient's pupils. 'Reacting to light. Respiratory function?'

'BP now one hundred over sixty,' the nurse said.

'Pulse is more stable.'

'Get those EEG leads back on and check electrolyte balance.'

'Hi, Stasy,' a young man said as he walked into the room. 'I heard you had a lovely problem for me.'

'Hi, Cliff. That was quick. Cliff's our general surgical consultant,' she said for Justin's benefit. The two men exchanged nods of acknowledgement. Stasy liked the general surgical consultant even though he looked as though he was about eighteen years old and far too young to be treating anyone. Instead, she knew he was only two years younger than herself and that his wife was expecting their first child.

'I was here for Alison's antenatal review. What's the situation?'

'Sixty-seven-year-old woman. Fell from a ladder,' Justin said before Stasy could answer. 'Possible punctured lung. Possible fracture to right hip, right ankle. Query on spinal injury. She's just starting to stabilise.'

'Pulse in her foot is getting stronger,' Stasy reported.

'Looks as though she's ready to go to X-Ray. The sooner we see what's happening, the better.'

'Right. Call me when you're ready,' Cliff said. 'I'll go back and check on my wife.'

'I take it you don't have a portable X-ray machine?' Justin asked.

'We do but it's currently in the neonatal department. The radiology department is just across the way.' Stasy pointed.

'Big enough to have a CT machine, small enough not to have multiple portable X-ray machines. Got it,' Justin remarked, as though he was sizing up the hospital.

'You're obviously from a big city hospital,' Stasy replied as they wheeled Mrs Ienfeld over to Radiology. Mrs Ienfeld was taken off their hands and they headed back to the nurses' station.

Justin nodded. 'Melbourne.'

'Too much pressure?'

'Pardon?'

Stasy shrugged. 'We've had a few doctors come through here for short periods of time because they needed a change of pace.'

'I don't need to destress,' he said quickly, although he could tell she didn't seem to believe him.

'That's what happened to Cliff. Too much stress.'

'Is he really qualified?' Justin couldn't help asking, and Stasy laughed. The sound, a nice lilting chuckle, caused Justin to smile. It had been a long time since he remembered anyone laughing in a hospital. It wasn't because he was stressed that he'd left his prominent position at Melbourne General to move to the small city of Mount Gambier. It wasn't because the workload had got to him or that he didn't get along with his colleagues.

Even so, he had to admit that the staff here were more relaxed and easy to relate to than the entire A and E department back in Melbourne. They knew their jobs, were professional and good at what they did but they obviously knew each other quite well. Personable. That was the word he'd use to describe this department and a lot of that credit would go to Stasy Roberts, even if she was just acting head of unit.

'He does have a baby face but, I assure you, he is qualified. He and his wife Alison were having trouble conceiving. Both of them, far too much stress. They left the city, came here for a twelve-month period and after they'd been here for eight months Alison managed to conceive. She's now in her final trimester and neither of them are planning to move from Mount Gambier.'

'Do you know this much about all of your colleagues?'

Stasy shrugged. 'Pretty much. That's the other thing about working in a smaller environment—you really get to know people. It's nice.'

'You don't find it intrusive?'

She laughed again. 'It's interesting that you see it as intrusive. We see it as working together like a well-oiled machine.' She sat down in a chair and indicated he should do the same. Justin decided to lean against the desk instead, crossing his arms over his chest. 'I guess you could say we're more…relaxed here. We generally know our patients quite well, having treated them for years, and as far as staff go, many of us have been here for well over a decade. When you work that long with people, you tend to get to know them quite well.'

'I guess it's something I'm going to have to get used to.'

'You didn't have your own band of merry men in Melbourne?' She raised her eyebrows as she spoke and Justin couldn't help smiling at her alliteration.

'I had my team but I can't say I knew as much about their personal lives as you know about Cliff's.'

'Fair enough. I guess it's something you'll get used to while you're here.'

Justin wasn't too sure about that and as they

were joined by Gene, the nice conversation he'd been enjoying with Stasy came to an end. As she spoke to the registrar, he took the opportunity to assess her.

Her blonde hair was pulled back into a ponytail and her blue eyes reminded him of the sky on a cloudless day. Bright and blue. She laughed at something Gene had said and he noticed the laughter lines around her eyes as though this was something she did quite often. Her fingers were devoid of jewellery but that didn't mean much. Many women either wore their rings on chains around their necks or left them at home. He himself didn't wear a ring but, then, he wasn't married. Not any more.

The phone rang and Stasy turned to answer it, watching out of the corner of her eye as Gene shook hands with Justin. She thought she heard the words 'honour' and 'terrific opportunity' but she couldn't be sure. What was Gene talking about? She turned her attention to the paramedic who was on the line, letting her know that one of the boys at Pemrose School had broken his leg and they were bringing him in.

'Who is it?' Stasy asked, her tone a little tense.

'Relax. It's not your son,' the paramedic told her. 'Liam Van Der Built. His mother's been contacted. She's going straight to the hospital. We'll see you in five.'

'Thanks.' Stasy finished writing down the information, requested the patient's notes to be pulled, then turned to face Justin and Gene who were deep in conversation about the latest issue of the *Journal of Emergency Medicine*. Stasy had her most recent copy by her bed to read but hadn't managed to get to it lately.

'It was a brilliant article,' Gene said.

'Thanks.' Justin accepted the praise and Stasy raised her eyebrows.

'You've had an article published in the *Journal*?'

Gene looked at her as though she had grown

an extra head and Justin nodded. 'I do. Who
was the phone call from?'

Stasy gave them both a rundown on the situation.

'It's not one of yours, is it?' Gene asked
before she could give him the name.

'No.'

'One of yours…what?' Justin asked.

'Stasy has twins,' Gene supplied.

'Almost nine-year-old twins and my son Tim
is…well, let's say he's a bit of an adventurer.
He's broken both arms—falling out of trees;
sustained a hairline fracture to his foot—skate-
boarding; and he broke his leg on the final day
of school last year because he was so excited
the year was over that he ran from the room,
tripped and took a tumble down the stairs.'

'He'd know the staff here better than you
do,' Justin remarked.

Stasy nodded and smiled. 'You've got that
right. Thankfully, the only medical concern
my daughter is likely to develop is buyers'

remorse, and I'm more than equipped to deal with that one.'

The sound of the ambulance's siren could be heard as it drew closer. Justin frowned.

'If they're only bringing in a boy with a broken leg, why do they have the sirens on?'

'Probably because Liam insisted.' She handed him the file on the eight-year-old boy.

Justin quickly scanned the file. 'He doesn't appear to have hurt himself before.'

'No, which is why a trip in the ambulance would be a real treat for him.'

'You said he goes to Pemrose School?'

'Yes.'

'Is that where your two go?' He looked at her.

'Yes. Why?'

'That's where my son goes. He started two weeks ago.'

Stasy absorbed the news that her new colleague had a son. She glanced briefly at his left hand but saw that he wore no wedding ring, not that that didn't mean he wasn't married. Many medical professionals didn't wear rings. She met his eyes. 'Let me guess. Your son is Mike?'

'Yes! How did you know?'

Stasy laughed. 'Mount Gambier is smaller than Melbourne, Justin. Small town, small school.' They headed out to the ambulance bay, waiting for the vehicle to come to a complete stop. She opened the back doors of the ambulance.

'Hello, Liam.'

'Hi, Stasy. Did you hear that I'd broken my leg?'

'I did. What on earth were you doing?'

'Uh…showing off on the monkey bars.'

'Monkey bars?' They took the paramedic stretcher into the hospital and transferred Liam to a bed. 'What exactly were you doing?'

'I was walking along the top of them and I…well, I sorta slipped.'

Stasy found it difficult not to smile and turned away. 'Well, at least all that appears to be wrong with you is a broken leg.'

'It says here,' Justin interjected, reading the paramedic's report, 'that you've had some midazolam. How are you feeling?'

'Super-fine.'

'I'll bet. I doubt your mother's going to be feeling super-fine when she gets here,' Stasy remarked as she checked Liam's pupils.

Justin wound the blood-pressure cuff around the boy's arm and when he announced it was fine, they checked his pulse points.

'Does she have to know?'

'Liam honey, we can't treat you unless she knows. We'll get you off to X-Ray and wait for your mum to arrive.'

Stasy took Liam to Radiology and received the films for Mrs Ienfeld, who was now stable and under constant bedside nursing in cubicle one. She returned to the nurses' station and took the films out, hooking them onto the viewing box.

'No damage to the spine, thank goodness.' She pointed to the area in question.

'Definite fracture to the right tib and fib and it looks as though she'll be needing a total hip replacement on the right side to match the one on her left,' Justin added.

'It looks as though she's been very lucky with that lung. Definitely blunt force trauma but the lining doesn't appear to have been punctured.'

'I'll give Cliff a call and he can take it from here.' Stasy organised the transfer of their patient then headed over to speak to Liam's mother, who had just arrived. As she spoke to her, she watched as Cliff came back into the department and shook hands with Justin, the two men talking animatedly together. It was strange. First Gene and now Cliff. Come to think of it, she'd also noticed a few of the nurses giving Justin interested looks but she'd just thought that had been because he was handsome.

Was she the only one who wasn't overawed by the new boss? Maybe it was just that? Maybe it was because he would now be head of A and E that staff were being overly attentive. It was strange because at such a small hospital people tended to be very relaxed, very informal, and not usually impressed by a doctor simply because he came from a big hospital in the city.

When Liam came back from Radiology, Stasy and Justin were pleased to report the fracture was merely a greenstick fracture, where the bone hadn't been fractured all the way through and that it could be fixed with a simple cast.

Justin offered to apply the cast. 'I haven't done such a simple job in such a long time,' he said as he wound the cotton around Liam's leg. Stasy watched him, under the guise of filling in the paperwork, noting the way he was relaxed and friendly with the boy. Well, seeing as he had a son around that age, it was no wonder he was good with children.

He laughed at something Liam said and Stasy liked the way his brown eyes twinkled.

There was no denying that he was indeed a handsome man but as he was no doubt married, that meant he was just another good-looking colleague she got to work with. Although those eyes…a woman could drown in those eyes. His brown hair was thick and wavy and she had no doubt that it would become quite unruly if he didn't keep it as short as he did.

She looked back to what she was supposed to be doing, wrote a few more lines and then signed her name. Excusing herself, she went back to the nurses' station where Gene and Cliff were talking.

'I didn't realise it was *him* straight away,' Cliff said.

'Didn't realise who was who?' Stasy asked.

'Justin.'

'What about Justin?'

Both men stared at her and again she had that feeling that something was wrong.

'Haven't you read your memos, Stasy?'

'You know paperwork is the last thing I get

around to dealing with, Gene,' she remarked. 'And now that Justin's here, he can have the lot.'

'You should have read your memos,' Cliff stated, and handed her a piece of paper. Stasy scanned the sheet, her eyes widening slowly as she read the information.

'Justin is Justin *Gray*? *The* Justin Gray? *Professor Justin Gray?* The man who has single handedly revolutionised techniques for emergency medicine for the past ten years?'

'Guilty as charged,' a deep voice said from behind her, and Stasy turned to look at the man in question, her eyes wide with shock.

CHAPTER TWO

'THEN what happened?' Skye sat perched on a bench stool as she watched her sister make dinner.

'I...I just stood there. Like an idiot. Swamped with mortification and embarrassment. You know those moments you have when you wish the ground would just open up and swallow you?'

'Yes?' Skye pinched a carrot stick and began to munch on it.

'Well, it was like that.' Stasy closed her eyes and shook her head at the memory. 'One little bit of paper. If I'd just read that one little piece of paper, I wouldn't have made such a fool of myself.'

'How did the dishy new doctor take it?'

'Justin? He was fine. He just laughed, told me

to forget it and we moved on but, oh, Skye, it's one of those key moments in a person's life which I will never be able to wipe from my memory. I've read this man's papers, I've pored over the textbooks he's written. My copy of his first book is so dog-eared I had to buy a new one. He's a genius!'

'Then what's he doing here?'

'I don't know. I also didn't know he had a son but he does. Perhaps he and his family wanted a change from the city.'

'Is he cute, though?'

'What's that got to do with it? He's a colleague and he's probably married.'

'So? Is he cute? Nothing wrong with having a bit of eye candy at work, sis.'

Stasy stopped stirring the pot of chili she was making and thought back to the way Justin Gray's eyes had made her feel the few times he'd looked her way. She'd caught him, once when she'd been talking to Gene and then a few minutes after she'd discovered his real identity.

Of course she'd told herself that he was most probably trying to size up whether or not she was a good doctor but it was just a feeling…just a strange sensation and one which made her feel more decidedly feminine than she'd felt in years.

'Well? It's not that difficult, Stase. He's either handsome or not.'

'Definitely handsome,' was the answer and she sighed before stirring the pot once more.

'Whoo-eee. By the way he seems to have you daydreaming, I'd say he's better than hand-some. And you don't know if he's married? Stase, you should find out.'

'Why? Even if he isn't, I'm not interested.'

'You should be. Stasy, it's been eight years since Wilt left.'

'I'm not interested,' she said with more force, hoping her sister would drop it.

'I finish my degree in four months' time and then I'll be working overseas. It'll just be you and the kids, and you and I both know it's not good for you to be on your own.'

'I'm fine, Skye. I'm a grown woman who's been a single parent for almost a decade. I think I can handle things. Besides, I won't be on my own. I have Tim and Chelsea.'

'I'm talking about adult companionship.'

'I get enough of that at work.'

'You can't fool me. I know you get lonely at night time. In fact, sometimes, when you wake me to tell me you've been called out, I can hear the excitement in your voice. It's like you finally have something to occupy your mind with.'

'So? I'm a doctor. It's good for me to be excited about my job.'

'I'm not saying it isn't.' Skye paused and looked intently at her. 'Since Mum and Dad died you've been more…I don't know…distant.'

'I miss them.'

'So do I and I'm forever grateful that you've let me come to stay with you for these past few years.'

'The arrangement works well for everyone. I support you in your studies and you help look after the kids while I'm working. Who better than their own aunt?'

'Stase, all I'm saying is don't close yourself off to the idea of perhaps meeting someone new and beginning a new life. Trust me. I've studied this. Psychology is my business. I know what I'm talking about and loneliness is…well, it's horrible and I don't want to see you going through that any more.'

The chili started bubbling and Stasy quickly returned her attention to it to make sure it didn't burn. 'Dinner's almost ready. Can you make sure the kids have finished their chores outside then get them to wash their hands, please?'

'Sure.' Skye took one more carrot stick as she slid from the stool, narrowly missing the swipe Stasy took at her for pinching food from the salad. 'You'll have to be faster than that, big sister.'

Stasy thought about her sister's words as she

sat in the lounge room later that evening. Both Tim and Chelsea were tucked up in bed and Skye, who lived in a small attached apartment they'd added onto the house a few years back, was busy studying.

Since their parents had died two years ago, Stasy had felt her shoulders becoming heavier as the weight of the world had seemed to settle there. Skye, who was almost ten years younger than her, had just started her second degree. The twins had still been settling in at school and she'd taken on the role of Acting Head of A and E. Every day she woke up, did what she had to do and then went to sleep at night.

Even now, sitting in the dark, watching the clock with its luminous display tick from one number to the next, Stasy wondered how her life had ended up this way. She'd once been fun, crazy, zany and now she was what? Mature? Adult? Professional? Turning forty in two years' time?

She closed her eyes and shook her head as

she recalled how unprofessional she'd been with Justin Gray. His face came easily to mind, which surprised her. The contours of his face, the lines she'd seen when he'd laughed, the rich colour of his eyes, the sureness of his hands as he'd dealt with their patients. The thoughts brought a smile to her face and a warmth to her heart which it hadn't felt in a very long time.

She idly wondered if those hands were as sure in other tasks they might perform. The instant the thought came, she pushed it away, astounded that she might be thinking about another woman's husband.

'Well, the least you can do tomorrow is find out whether he's married or not,' she told herself as she stood and headed for her bedroom. If he wasn't, she might even give herself permission to daydream a little…but only a little.

The morning brought the usual rush, in getting the twins up and ready for school, making lunches for everyone, ensuring her son finished all his breakfast and getting out meat to defrost for the evening meal.

'How did you sleep?' Skye asked Stasy as she finished ironing a shirt.

Stasy pulled a face and waved her hand in the so-so gesture.

'That good, eh?' Skye's eyes twinkled with teasing. 'Didn't...*dream* about anyone, did you?'

'No.' Stasy was too quick to deny it and knew her sister had picked up on it.

'No handsome new doctors to fill your sub-conscious?'

'Skye!' Stasy put her hands on her hips as Chelsea came in to the room.

'Ooh she's mad at you, Aunty Skye,' she crooned.

'Glad it's not me,' Tim said as he packed his schoolbag.

'Right. We're leaving in five minutes,' Stasy called as Skye giggled before leaving the room. Stasy unplugged the iron and glanced out the window. Rain again. 'Make sure you have your wet-weather gear,' she warned her children. 'It looks like another rainy day ahead.'

They all headed out and after Stasy had dropped the children at their school, watching as they raced inside to get out of the rain, she headed for the university.

'So, did you dream about him?'

'Skye.' Stasy sighed but looked over at her sister briefly. She was grinning wildly and Stasy could only laugh. 'If I did it doesn't mean anything.'

'Of course it does. It means you're attracted to him.'

'He might be married.'

'Why don't you ask him?'

'I couldn't do that!'

'Why not? You know, just casually ask him how his wife is settling into her new life here in Mount Gambier. It's quite innocent when you do it like that.'

Stasy pulled the car up at the university gates.

'Good bye, little sister. Enjoy a nice long day of lectures.' As she drove to the hospital, she remembered her resolve of the night before, that being to find out if Justin Gray was married. It was strange that the information should be so important but the fact of the matter was that she *had* dreamt about him last night. She'd woken that morning and wondered why on earth she'd fantasised about him holding her, laughing at her jokes, kissing her.

She wasn't even remotely interested in finding a man. She didn't have time for that in her life…even if sharing the evenings, sharing her life with a man was something she had missed. She'd been on her own for too long and was probably too stuck in a rut to even think about dating again. Oh, she'd tried it a few years after Wilt had left but nothing had worked out. Skye had told her more than once that she should move on with her life instead of just circling around, wondering where she should land. The question was, could she? Could she really do it? Get involved in someone else's life? Let them be a part of hers?

The instant she set foot inside the hospital the first person she saw was Justin, and a wave of apprehension washed over her. She quickly reminded herself that he had no idea what she'd dreamt about so she should just control herself and be the professional he no doubt expected her to be.

'Good morning, Professor,' she said brightly as she walked in.

Justin looked up, from where he was writing notes, slightly embarrassed. 'Don't call me that. Here I'm just Justin.'

'You're Professor Gray. I may not have read the memo, I may have made a fool of myself yesterday, but the fact remains that you have one of the best brains in the world when it comes to emergency medicine and you deserve the title.'

He put down his pen and leaned back in the chair. 'Firstly, you did not make a fool of yourself yesterday and, secondly, I actually don't hold the title of Professor any more. That title is given to a person who lectures at a university. I'm no longer attached to any university so…' He shrugged as he trailed off.

'You'd only have to snap your fingers to have an offer to lecture here. The uni would be glad to have you as part of their faculty.'

Justin acknowledged her words with a slight inclination of his head. 'True, but that's not what I'm here for.' He watched with interest as she put her briefcase on the floor, then began to take off her scarf and coat and decided he was more than happy to give Stasy Roberts his undivided attention. Today she was dressed in black trousers and a pink shirt which really enhanced the blueness of her eyes. Her hair was back in an out-of-the-way ponytail but he could see that the ends were curling and still slightly damp from her morning shower. She smelt of roses and sunshine and as it was currently cold and raining, it was a welcome reprieve.

During the previous evening, he'd found his thoughts turning to her more than once and it had been on the tip of his tongue to ask his mother all about his new colleague. Of course, if he *had* asked, his mother would have wanted to know why and would, no doubt, have started matchmaking them at the first opportunity.

It may be just over three years since his wife, Rose, had died, but Justin hadn't even contemplated starting to date again. In fact, Stasy Roberts was the first woman who'd caught his interest and that alone had stunned him.

'Well, if that's not what you're here for, and you don't need to destress, what prompted the change to Mount Gambier?'

He smiled at that. He was as curious about her as she appeared to be about him. Was that a good thing or not? 'Are you always this nosy?'

'This is nosy? Getting to know a new colleague is now classified as being nosy?'

'Hmm. How does your husband put up with it?' he asked, hoping he wasn't being too obvious.

'I'm divorced,' she said quickly, her heartrate starting to increase. Why had he asked
her that? Did those little glances she'd inter-
cepted from him yesterday actually mean
more than she'd thought? She felt her mouth
go dry for a moment before she swallowed.
'Almost eight years now.' Why had she told
him that? He didn't need to know that but it
was too late now. It was out there. 'Uh…' She
started to fidget with the end of her scarf,
feeling self-conscious. He was watching her
closely and she looked away for a moment,
hoping her tone sounded equally as impersonal and not at all curious as she ventured,
'How about you?'

'How about me…what?'

'Uh…' Stasy gave a nervous laugh. 'Oh I just
meant are you married? You don't wear a ring
but, then, a lot of doctors don't.' She met his eyes
and could see the corners were tugging up as he
began to smile. 'Not that it's an issue if you are.
I mean…' She stopped and exhaled, forcing

herself to calm down. She was so transparent. No doubt he thought her a complete loon.

'I'm not married,' he finally said, and she wondered whether he'd enjoyed her discomfort. 'I'm a widower.'

'Oh.' Her tone was filled with sympathy and surprise. 'I'm sorry. I didn't mean to pry.'

'Yes, you did.' He closed the file before him and stood, carrying it over to the out-tray. 'You told me you were being nosy.'

'Actually, I denied that. I said I was just getting to know my new colleague.' Stasy was busy trying not to breathe in his rich, spicy scent which had floated her way when he'd moved past her.

'And how do you feel you're getting on?' He turned as he spoke and looked intently at her. His eyes were so vibrant, so hypnotic that for a moment Stasy found it difficult to breathe at all. Add to that fact his words could be taken in a completely different way and she wasn't at all sure which way was up!

The phone rang but neither of them moved. 'Saved by the bell.' Justin continued to hold her gaze as he leaned across to answer the phone.

'Dr Gray,' he said into the receiver.

It was enough to break Stasy out of the trance he'd woven around her and she quickly picked up her belongings and headed for her office. Once there, she closed the door behind her, leaning against it and trying to make her heartrate return to normal.

Had Justin Gray—correction, the *amazing* Professor Gray she'd held in such high professional esteem for most of her career—just been flirting with her? If he had, what did it mean? She now knew he wasn't married so it didn't matter if she dreamed about about him any more.

'Yes, it does,' she chided as she headed over to her desk, hanging up her coat and scarf as she went. After unloading her briefcase, she sat down behind her desk and looked at the large amount of paper in her in-tray.

She picked up a handful and started to sort through it, looking only for the memo that announced Justin's appointment. Although she'd read it yesterday, she wanted to see it again, shaking her head at being so thick. The minutes of the last board meeting were also included in her papers and as she read through them, she noted that Justin's presence was announced, as was the date he would start work at the hospital.

There was a knock at her door and before she could say anything, the door opened and Justin came in.

'Not bothering you, am I?'

For a moment Stasy wasn't quite sure how to answer that because, mentally and physically, he was definitely starting to bother her and she wasn't at all sure what to do about it. It had been far too many years since she'd experienced these sorts of emotions and she couldn't remember how to deal with them.

'Uh…no.'

He raised his eyebrows at her words as

though he didn't believe her but he came in and sat down opposite her. 'Christine said now might be a good time for you and I to discuss departmental business, while A and E is relatively quiet.'

Stasy's answer was to pick up the rest of her full in-tray and dump it down in front of him. 'Handover complete. Enjoy.'

Justin laughed and the sound washed over her like a comfortable, warm blanket. He pointed to the handful of papers in front of her. 'Don't I get those, too?'

'These are just the minutes of the last board meeting and as you were there, you know what happened.'

'Still beating yourself up about not knowing I was coming?'

Stasy shrugged. 'I should have known.'

'And would you have done anything differently?'

She thought on that for a moment. 'I'm not sure but at least I wouldn't have been standing

there looking like a goldfish yesterday afternoon when I eventually *did* find out.'

Justin smiled at the memory. 'I don't know.
I thought it was a good goldfish impersona-
tion.'

Stasy laughed and shook her head. 'Fair
enough. Well, perhaps we should move on
and get down to sorting out the mess you've
inherited.'

'Sounds like a good idea.'

They worked together for the next two hours,
making a lot of headway through the jungle of
administration.

'Coffee?' she asked when she finally put
her pen down.

'Definitely. Please, tell me, *please*, tell me
this hospital has more than just instant coffee?'
They both stood and headed for the door, Stasy
smiling as they walked to the kitchenette.

'Drip coffee is about the best we can do.'

'That's fine. Great in fact,' he said as she
poured two cups.

'Milk? Sugar?'

'Just sugar, thanks.'

She added sugar to his and milk to her own before carrying them to the table where they both sat down. 'So, Stasy, in the get-to-know-your-colleagues-better game, how long have you been working here?'

'Feels like for ever. I did all of my training here, apart from spending six months in Adelaide as part of my rotation.'

'Have you stayed in one place because of your kids?'

'Mainly. They need stability but, then, so did I.'

'And what about family support?'

'My sister lives with me. How about you? Do you have family here?'

'Yes. My parents are here. That's the main reason why I chose to move to Mount Gambier.'

'I did wonder. I mean, a man with your expertise and qualifications, well, you could have any job in the world you wanted.'

'Perhaps I've had enough of being the professor?'

'It's not a state of mind, Justin. You *are*
Professor Gray whether you're attached to a
university or not. You've inspired so many
students, interns, registrars, surgeons. You've
paved the way, guided many of us through difficult questions and earned the respect of every
medical professional who's ever read one of
your articles or one of your textbooks.'

He shrugged and took a sip of his coffee but
Stasy could see that her words had touched
him.

Stasy finished her own drink, unsure what
else to say. 'So, Professor, are you ready to get
back to work?'

'Ready as I'll ever be.'

As they headed back to her office, Stasy
asked, 'So who are your parents?'

'Ah, I was wondering when you were going
to ask, although I thought perhaps you'd
figured it out.'

'Gray. Gray.' She repeated his surname, hoping to get her mind into gear. Whose surname was Gray? She stopped. 'Oh, my goodness. You're Katherine and Herb's son!'

'Well done, Dr Roberts. I figured you'd know them.'

'And quite well, too. I also knew their son was a doctor but had no idea you were *that* Professor Gray. Anyway, your mum sometimes looks after the kids for me when my sister Skye's unavailable.' They walked into her office and Stasy shook her head. 'My mind must have been somewhere else for the past few weeks because I do remember Katherine telling me that her son and grandson had come to live here. In fact…' She paused for a moment. 'You're actually *living* with them, right?'

'That's right. Their house is so big and the four of us fit quite comfortably. Mike has someone there in the evenings if I'm called to the hospital so it works out well. Although—' he leaned a little closer and Stasy found herself mimicking the action '—I never thought I'd still be living at home when I was forty-two.'

Stasy leaned back and laughed. 'Has it been a big adjustment?'

Gee, she had a nice laugh. 'Not really.'

'They don't give you curfews or ask you who you were out late with?'

'I hope not.'

'Not a party animal, Professor?'

He raised his eyebrow at the title but let it slide. It wasn't mean or condescending when she said it and it wasn't as though she was calling him by his title either. When Stasy said it, especially with her lips twitching into a smile, it seemed to be more of nickname than anything else and Justin found he liked it.

'Hardly. I'm a workaholic.'

'That's right.' She nodded. 'The man who works full time, writes medical textbooks and raises a child. Quite the accomplished man, I must say.'

'Thank you.'

Her smile started to fade as she looked at him, her eyes intense. 'How did you do it?'

Justin thought for a moment before shrugging. 'I don't know. I've only written articles since my wife's death. Mike's taken up a lot of my free time—not that I begrudge him that but…' Justin trailed off and Stasy saw him put up a 'no trespassing' sign. 'Anyway, we should get back to work.'

'We should.' And that's what they did for another few hours. Finally her in-tray was clear and Justin had a small pile of paper before him.

'I take it I have secretarial support?'

'Three days a week. Wednesday, Thursday and Friday.'

'OK.' He flicked a finger over the papers. 'Looks as though my new secretary isn't going to like me much when she finds most of this waiting for her tomorrow morning.'

'She'll get a shock all right, especially considering she's usually begging me *for* work.'

As Justin stood, picking up the pile, Stasy went around to open the door for him. *'Adios!'*

'Is that to me or the papers?'

'The papers, of course. Now that this hospital has captured you, we're never going to let you go.'

He stepped a little closer, right into her comfort zone, and she was immediately surrounded by that hypnotic scent of his. He arched an inquisitive eyebrow and kept his eyes trained on hers.

'Is that a promise, Anastasia?'

CHAPTER THREE

JUSTIN walked wearily into his parents' home just after eight o'clock with a briefcase full of files.

'Is that you, dear?' Katherine called.

'Yes.' He put his things down and took off his coat and scarf, stopping momentarily on his way to the kitchen to warm his hands at the living-room fire. He kissed his mother's cheek. 'Something smells good. I thought you would have eaten by now.'

'We have. I've kept you a plate of food. Go say hi to Mike and I'll get it ready for you.'

'Where is he?'

Katherine gave him a level look. 'Where do you think he is? Hibernating in his room, where he usually goes after dinner.'

Justin nodded. 'I'll go say hi.' He headed up the stairs and knocked twice on Mike's door, waiting for permission to enter. It was still something new he was getting used to but his mother had told him to respect Mike's privacy so that was what he was doing. 'Mike?' he called when there was no answer. 'It's Dad. Can I come in?'

'Sure.'

It wasn't much but it was better than a negative answer. Justin pushed open the door to find his son sitting on the bed, holding something in his hands. It was an envelope. He walked over and sat on the bed, not too close so he didn't crowd Mike. 'How was today?'

Mike shrugged. 'OK.'

'Need help with your homework?'

'Nope.'

Justin tried not to sigh with despondencey. Mike had become increasingly withdrawn over the last three years. It was as though the older he got, the more he understood of his mother's death. Justin guessed there was quite a bit of difference between the way a six-year-old and nine-year-old dealt with grief.

In Melbourne, Justin had tried several things to try and help Mike to deal with things. He'd cut back on his working hours, taking himself off night shift altogether, hiring a housekeeper to not only make sure the house was tidy but so they both ate decent meals. She'd also been there when Mike had come home from school so that he hadn't been there alone.

Justin had taken him on a holiday to Queensland where they'd enjoyed riding the roller-coasters at the theme parks as well as walking along the beaches but nothing had seemed to work. He'd be happy for a short time then it was as though reality returned and Mike would slip back into a world where it was becoming increasingly difficult for Justin to reach him.

When Rose had died, both of their worlds had been ripped apart, but where Justin, being the adult, had worked steadily through his grief, Mike seemed to be hoarding it. Justin knew his son would eventually crack and he was trying to do whatever he could to lessen the aftershocks. Mike also seemed to be avoiding getting close to anyone else, including his grandparents.

That was the report Justin had received from the one session of grief counselling he'd managed to get Mike to attend. The boy didn't want to get too close to anyone in case they died, too. It was a protective reflex and one which was not only quite common but would simply take time and reassurance to overcome.

Justin pointed to the envelope in Mike's hands. 'What's that?'

'An invitation.'

'Yeah? What for?'

'Birthday party. Some kids at school are having a birthday party this weekend and I've been invited.'

Justin was surprised and thankful at the same time. 'Well, that's good, right? May I have a look?' Perhaps getting Mike to interact with new children, with kids who hadn't known his mother, was starting to pay off. A fresh start was what Justin had hoped for by moving here, as well as providing Mike with extra support from Katherine and Herb. Was this the beginning?

Mike handed the envelope over and when his eyes met his father's, Justin was relieved to see a tiny spark of life beginning to flare within. When he opened it, he realised it was from Stasy's twins.

'Tim and Chelsea, eh?'

'Yeah. They're in my class.'

Ah. No wonder Stasy had been able to figure out Mike's name the other day. Her kids had obviously told her about a new boy from Melbourne. 'It's nice of them to invite you.'

'Tim told me he really wants me to come. Tim said he has a big back yard and even has a real, honest tree-house.' The spark of life became brighter.

'Does he, now?' Justin read the address and tried to remember where that was. It had been over twenty years since he'd last lived in Mount Gambier and, as far as he could recall, the area where Stasy lived had all been farmland.

'Do you want to go?'

Mike shrugged, trying not to show that he cared, but Justin could tell that he really did. 'I guess so. It says that parents can come, too. Tim said his mum likes to have big barbecues with everyone coming over, and she reckons it's the easiest way to have a party for twins.'

Justin smiled because he could picture Stasy saying something like that. How surprising that he seemed so in tune with her so quickly.

'What's so funny?'

'Nothing.' Justin handed the invitation back to him. 'I think it sounds like fun. Have you told Tim you'll come?'

'I can go?' There was that light again in his eyes.

'Sure. I'm not working either so I'm more than happy to take you.'

'What about Gran and Grandpa?'

'Do you want them to come?'

He shrugged again. 'Guess so. Do you think they want to?'

It was a step. Justin knew it was a big step and he wanted to grab his little boy into his arms and hug him tight, to let him know he was proud of him for taking this step, but at the same time he knew such an action would only make Mike withdraw. He was trying to reach out to his grandparents and if Stasy had been standing before him, Justin would have kissed her for allowing her children to have a party where they could invite their friends.

'I think they'd definitely go if you asked them.'

'Can't you do it?'

Justin tapped the envelope. 'Your invitation. Your job.'

'What do I do? How do I, you know, ask them?'

'Why not show Gran and Grandpa the

invite, let them read it then ask them if they want to go?'

'Will you come with me?'

Justin's smile was broad and, unable to contain himself any longer, he reached out and ruffled his son's hair. 'You betcha.'

'Stasy,' Justin called as he came out of his office the following morning.

'Hi, Justin.' Stasy tried not to blush when she saw him. This was mainly because she'd had another night where he'd visited her in her dreams and now that she knew he was unattached, her subconscious had gone wild.

'Can you come in to my office for a moment?'

'Sure. Just give me a sec.' She quickly unlocked her office and dumped her things before stepping next door into his room. 'Problem? Has the secretary quit?'

His smile was quick. 'No. Uh…I just wanted to say thank you for getting Tim to ask Mike to the party this weekend.'

'I didn't get Tim to do it. Tim *wanted* to do it, Justin. He likes Mike. In fact, all I heard about yesterday was how cool Mike was and how they chased the girls together at lunchtime and how fast Mike could run and how good Mike was at maths. In fact, I'm getting quite sick of hearing how brilliant your son is, Professor.' She smiled as she spoke, and Justin could see that bright, teasing light in her eyes. She looked dazzling. Beautiful and dazzling.

Today she was wearing a pair of navy trousers and a dark green top and he could have sworn her eyes had changed colour. They certainly looked green today. He frowned.

'I was just kidding,' she pointed out when his expression changed.

He took a step closer and looked more intently into her eyes.

Stasy swallowed, trying not to be affected by the warmth emanating from his body. His gaze was so intense, though, she began to squirm a little, feeling self-conscious.

'Justin?'

'Your eyes are green.'

She looked at him in surprise at the unexpected comment. The tension that had started to build at his intense scrutiny began to lift but the feelings evoked by the nearness of his body stayed. 'They're blue,' she said.

'I could have sworn they were blue but today they're decidedly green.'

'Ever heard of coloured contact lenses?' In some ways, she wished she hadn't spoken because at her words he straightened up but didn't step back.

'Were you wearing blue ones yesterday?'

'Yes.'

'What other colours do you have?'

'Only blue and green.'

'They're prescription?'

'Yes.'

'So you wear glasses?'

'Well…not when I'm wearing the contacts, obviously.'

'Obviously.' He smiled at that and moved around the office, sitting behind his desk.

'What about you?' she asked. 'Do you wear glasses? Contacts?' She knew he didn't wear contacts because, after looking into his gorgeous brown eyes as she just had, she would have seen them. No, he was all natural. Gorgeous and natural.

'No. I have perfect vision. My mother says I should have been a pilot.'

Stasy smiled and nodded. 'I can hear your mum saying something like that. Thank goodness you didn't listen to her because the medical profession would have been poorer for it. So, anyway, are you all coming on Saturday?'

He was touched by her words. It wasn't the first time she'd said something like that and it was clear she meant it, clear she appreciated his contribution, and he'd never been more glad he'd chosen medicine as his profession. Other colleagues had put him so far up on a pedestal he'd had a difficult time relating to them.

Again, it was the difference between a large hospital and a small one. Or perhaps it was the difference between a person who was grounded, like Stasy, and someone who was impressed with titles. 'Are we coming? Most definitely. It's really brightened Mike up.'

Stasy was alert to his words. 'He's been having problems? I guess it's difficult, settling into a new town, new school,' she continued, answering her own question.

'Yes.' Justin was more than happy to leave it at that for now.

'Well, glad we could be of service and, seriously, Tim and Chelsea have given out the invitations on their own so who knows who's going to turn up?'

'Do you need to organise security?'

She laughed at that. 'This is Mount Gambier, Justin. Not Melbourne. Besides, my friends Brad and Marie will be there. They're both police officers so we should be right as far as security goes.'

'Always good to invite the police to your parties.'

'Exactly.' They both smiled at each other and she was so glad he was on her wavelength. Their humour appeared to be quite similar and she liked it. 'Was there anything else?' She indicated the very neat, very organised desk he sat behind. 'Apart from polishing your desk until you can see your face reflected in it?'

'What?'

'Nothing.' She waved her words away. 'It's just that your desk is so neat and mine's so…well, you can't even see what sort of wood my desk is made from *and* you've taken most of the work from it.'

'Does the old saying, "Messy desk, messy mind" apply to you?'

'I hope not. Besides, I thought it was "Messy desk, warm heart".'

'No. That's "Cold hands, warm heart".'

'Well, who knows?' Stasy threw her hands in the air. 'I'm a doctor, not a quotation dictionary.'

'Quite true.'

'So I take it you've managed to get through all that work already?'

'Basically.'

'How do you do it?'

'Methodically,' he answered. 'I took it home last night and worked on it after everyone had gone to bed.'

'Well, you did tell me you were a workaholic so I guess I shouldn't have expected anything less. Or is it that you're an insomniac as well?'

'No.' Although he had experienced a bit of trouble settling his mind last night, mainly due to thoughts of the woman before him. She'd obviously been through a lot. She said she'd been divorced for almost eight years and her children were about to turn nine which meant she'd been raising twins on her own as well as working at the hospital. That took a lot of inner strength and his admiration for her continued to grow the more they became acquainted.

The phone on his desk rang and he answered

it, waving to Stasy as she left his room. A minute later he was walking with her down the corridor towards A and E, the call having been from Christine, saying they were both needed.

'Who's injuring themselves this early on a Wednesday morning?' Justin asked, trying not to be distracted by Stasy's fresh scent. The ambulance was now right outside the door so it appeared they didn't have long to wait until they found out.

Christine reported that a ten-year-old boy had been involved in a motor vehicle accident on the way to school.

'Father was driving the car and is thankfully only dazed but the accident impact was on the front passenger side.'

'No airbags?' Justin asked.

Christine shook her head. 'Old car.'

Stasy went to the sink to wash her hands before pulling on a pair of gloves as the boy was wheeled in. These were the sorts of accidents she found the most difficult to deal with, given that her children were around the same age as this boy. She heard Justin and the paramedics transfer the patient to the hospital bed and when she looked over at the supine form, she froze for a second, thinking how small he looked with the oxygen non-rebreather mask over his face, neck brace securing his spine and his school clothes all bloodied and torn.

'You all right?' Justin's tone was soft as he stood by her side, his warmth surrounding her.

She looked up at him and saw compassion in his eyes. 'Yes. Thanks for checking, though.'

'It's difficult when they're the same age as your own kids. Let's focus and get to work.'

'Patient's name is Benjamin Litchfield. Possible fracture to left tibia and fibula, left radius and ulna, temporary loss of consciousness due to possible head injury. Midazolam administered at accident site.' While the paramedic read out the report, Christine and her staff were cutting off Benjamin's clothes so they could get a better look at the injury sites.

Stasy attached ECG leads and an oximeter.

'I'll want an EEG reading, too,' Justin instructed as he leaned over Benjamin, checking the boy's pupils. 'Ben? Ben? Can you hear me?' There was no response. 'Pupils equal and reacting to light.' Justin continued his Glasgow coma scale assessment, checking Benjamin's reaction to stimulation.

'Benjamin?' Stasy said loudly but firmly, using her best 'motherly' voice. 'Wake up, Benjamin.'

He stirred this time. 'Mum?' The word was barely a whisper but it was a reply nevertheless.

'Proof of yet another boy who's nagged by his mum in the mornings.' Justin looked at Stasy and winked. 'Good work.'

Stasy was completely captivated for a second or two. Justin had just winked at her! A noise behind her startled her thoughts back into place and she looked down at her patient. 'Don't fret, Benjamin. Just lie still,' she said when he tried to open his eyes. 'Do you know where you are?'

Benjamin shifted, trying to move, but only

ended up moaning in pain. 'You have a brace around your neck, sweetheart,' Stasy said. 'Lie still. Are you in pain?'

Benjamin's bottom lip began to wobble and the small 'yes' that came from his lips, accompanied by a solitary tear which rolled down his cheeks, melted Stasy's heart.

'Oh, sweetheart.' She reached for a tissue and dabbed at his eyes. 'It's going to be all right. We'll give you something for the pain. Get you comfortable.' She turned to Christine and gave instructions for analgesics before returning her attention to Benjamin. 'Do you know where you are?' she asked again.

'Hospital,' came the whispered reply.

'Yes, you are. Good boy. Do you remember what happened?'

'No.'

Stasy kept on with her observations while the nurses drew up the drug she'd ordered and administered it through the IV line. 'There you go. That should feel better now.'

'He'll need X-rays of the left arm and leg as well as the skull.' Justin held out his hand for the forms and wrote up the request. He then performed the test for Babinski's sign by running the reflex hammer up the soles of Benjamin's feet. The toes on both feet curled, letting Justin know there was no damage to the motor system above the level of the spinal nerves.

'Patient hasn't voided,' Christine reported.

'Bladder rupture could be a possibility.'

'Analgesics are working,' Stasy commented as Benjamin closed his eyes and relaxed. She brushed some hair back from his head while Justin checked the reports from the machines.

'Good. We'll get someone from Urology to have a look at him, as well as an ortho registrar.'

'I'll get his transfer organised,' Stasy said as Christine checked Benjamin's neurological observations again.

'Transfer?'

'This isn't a big city hospital, Justin.' She reminded him with a small smile. 'We can stabilise Benjamin but he'll no doubt need an operation and we really only have elective lists here.'

'Oh, yeah.'

'You've got to change your way of thinking, city boy.' Her eyes were twinkling as she teased him.

'I'm working on it.'

'BP is low,' Christine said.

'Get a litre of saline going,' Justin ordered. 'I'll get this gash on Ben's leg sorted out.' The nurse administered a local anaesthetic and while he waited for it to take effect, Justin pulled out the items he'd need. Stasy watched as he opened a few cupboards, searching for what he needed, but he found everything with ease and she knew that in time he'd come to learn where things were kept. This was only his third day in the hospital and yet it somehow seemed as though he'd been here for a lot longer.

Or was it just that since she'd met him her life had become more…interesting? She thought about him at night, she couldn't wait to see him at work and there definitely appeared to be something beginning to brew between them. Was it just a comfortable working friendship? No. It was more than that and she wasn't sure how that made her feel. There'd be time enough for self-analysis later, she said to herself, but still, she couldn't stop thinking about him.

He was charming, handsome and funny. Skye would tell her that men like that didn't grow on trees and Stasy knew her sister was right, but Justin, no doubt, had his own problems to deal with and she had hers.

She watched what he was doing as he debrided the small gash then began to stitch it up. 'Nice needlework,' she commented.

'Thanks. I used to be in a quilting group back in Melbourne.'

'Seriously?' She looked at him in total surprise.

Justin merely gave her a look that told her instantly that he'd been joking.

'Oh, very funny.'

'I thought so.'

Benjamin began to stir just as Justin finished. Christine applied a fresh bandage to the wound site and Stasy looked down at the little boy. He was so young, so small, and while it sometimes felt like they grew up overnight, she knew when they were like this, they were as fragile as newborns.

'Where's my dad?' he asked, fighting back tears.

'He's on his way in, Ben,' she told him gently. 'He'll be here soon.'

'We were in the car,' Benjamin said in a whisper. 'I looked out the window and there was this car and then…' Tears began to seep out of his eyes and Stasy dabbed them away.

'Shh. It's all right, sweetheart. Your dad will be here soon and you're going to be fine.'

'Do I need to have an operation?'

'Yes. We're going to send you to Adelaide to one of the big hospitals there and they'll take care of you.'

The lower lip wobbled again. 'Can my dad come?'

As Benjamin spoke, Stasy heard voices outside the room and looked up to see a frantic man heading towards them. Justin spoke to the man and a moment later both of them came into the room.

'Here's your dad, mate,' Justin told Benjamin. Stasy stepped back from the bed and watched as the poor father, who looked as though he'd aged ten years in ten minutes, came and kissed his son's head.

She was standing next to Justin and for a few seconds both of them simply stood there, taking in the emotional sight of father and son.

'Good to see,' Justin murmured in her ear, and it was then Stasy realised just how close he was.

She angled her head up and for a second gazed longingly at his lips, recalling the dreams she'd had for the past two nights and how, in those dreams, Justin had pressed his mouth tenderly to her own.

Forcing her mind back to the present, she swallowed over the sudden dryness of her throat. 'You're a firm believer in family, then?'

He nodded, still looking at the touching scene. 'It's why I've moved back home. Mike needs more stability. More…family.' His words had slowed and he turned his head, capturing her gaze with his own. Stasy felt her body flood with tingles of excitement and apprehension before she finally summoned the strength to tear her eyes away.

CHAPTER FOUR

'AND?' Skye demanded that evening, when Stasy told her about the time-standing-still moment she'd shared with Justin.

'And what?'

'Ugh. You are so frustrating. What happened next? Did he say anything? Did he try and kiss you? *What?*'

'Someone's kissing Mum?' Chelsea's eyes were wide as she came into the room, her brother hard on her heels. 'Have you got a boyfriend, Mum?'

'Aw. Gross,' Tim said. 'Girls. Kissing. Yuck. I'm never gonna kiss a girl. I might chase them but I'm never gonna kiss them.'

'You kiss me,' Chelsea pointed out. 'And Aunty Skye and Mum.'

'That's different, dummy. You're family. Other girls…' He shuddered at the thought. 'Yuck.'

'Can I get that in writing?' Stasy asked. 'It'll save me a lot of heartache later on.' Skye laughed and the kids looked at her as though she were speaking another language. Personally, Stasy was glad the question Chelsea had initially asked had been totally ignored. 'Dinner's almost ready. Have you fed the animals?'

'Yes, Mum,' they both replied.

'Right. Go wash your hands. Skye, set the table, please.'

The twins walked out of the room but Skye didn't move. 'I'm not doing anything until you tell me what happened.'

'Nothing happened.' Stasy spread her arms wide. 'It was a moment. It was just a…fleeting, passing, wonderful, tremulous moment. Nothing more.'

'So what? You just stared at each other and then walked away?'

'We were attending to a patient, Skye. There were other people in the room.'

'You so wanted him to kiss you, though. At least admit that.' Skye gathered up the cutlery and walked across to the table, which wasn't too far from the compact country kitchen Stasy loved to cook in.

'Skye!'

'What? What's wrong with wanting a handsome doctor to kiss you? You're living in the past, sis. You have to move on.'

'I have moved on.'

'Not in the way I'm meaning.'

Stasy sighed and closed her eyes for a moment. 'I know.'

'You do? You didn't two days ago.'

'I know. It's as though meeting Justin has changed everything.' She shrugged and pulled the plates out, starting to dish up. 'We get along well, we work well together.'

'You're both attracted to each other.'

'I don't know about that.'

'Well, *you're* attracted to him. At least admit that much.'

'He's a good-looking, successful, single man. What woman *wouldn't* be attracted?'

'Is he coming to the party with his son?'

'Yes.'

Skye clapped her hands. 'Goody. I can't wait to meet the man who's unhinged my sister a bit.'

'I'm not unhinged.'

'No? It's a compliment, darling. It's fantastic to see you even contemplating another man. I never thought you'd be able to move on from Wilt.'

'Oh, I don't love Wilt. I haven't been carrying a torch for my ex-husband for all these years if that's what you're thinking. I'm simply not into having my heart ripped out and cut into a gazillion pieces again.'

'Come on. You don't know that's going to happen this time around.'

'It might. Plus I have the children to protect.'

'What if things work out, though? Have you ever thought of it that way? What if this Justin is the right man for you?'

'What if he's not? Look, Skye, it's ridiculous arguing semantics when there's nothing between us but professional joviality.'

'Professional what?' Skye couldn't help but laugh at her sister. 'Oh, Stase. You do have it bad.'

'Have what bad?'

'Don't worry about it,' Skye continued, ignoring her. 'Leave everything to me.'

Thankfully, when Saturday dawned, for the first time in weeks the sun was out and the rain had all but disappeared. Sure, the ground was still soggy and wet but Stasy could cope with that. The twins were both hyperactive and eager to help get set up for the party, and by the time the first of the guests started to arrive the back yard as well as the house was decorated with balloons, streamers and other party favours.

Stasy watched eagerly as each car came down her muddy driveway, anticipation mounting in the hope that it was Justin, only to be disappointed when it wasn't him. She scolded herself. Telling herself not to worry, not to fret. He would come. He'd said he would.

They'd both been quite busy for the past few days at the hospital and now that she'd officially handed over the reins, she couldn't even delay him under the guise of paperwork. They hadn't shared any more alarmingly unnerving moments like the one they'd experienced on Wednesday and although Stasy was thankful for that, it hadn't diminished his role during her evening subconscious ramblings.

It was the strangest thing in the world because she wasn't looking for a man, hadn't even considered the possibility of dating. Instead, she'd constantly told herself that her life was full enough—which it was but somehow meeting Justin and enjoying his presence had shown her there were a few cracks here and there. Since meeting him, her nights had been a mixture of loneliness and confusion as she'd found herself reliving conversations they'd had. The way he smiled made her stomach do flip-flops and that was something that hadn't happened in a very long time. The way his crisp workshirts outlined and hinted at his toned and firm physique beneath almost drove her to distraction. The way his laugh washed over her, making her feel young, free and very special.

She had no idea how he did it, how he affected her so completely and in such a short time when she hadn't been wanting anything new. Skye had often said that one day she'd meet someone else and—bam! It would be like she'd been hit by a truck. Was that what was happening here? Was Justin her truck?

'Hi.'

Stasy turned, surprised to find Justin standing

behind her. 'Hi,' she replied eagerly. 'You're here.' She looked at the driveway, then back to him. 'I didn't see you arrive.'

'I came with my parents,' he said, and shrugged. 'Seemed silly to bring two cars.' He smiled, thinking how it seemed silly to stand there in the presence of such beauty and not appreciate it either. Stasy was wearing flat walking boots, denim jeans and a warm cable-knit jumper…and her hair was loose. The blonde strands were being blown gently around her face and shoulders and when she shifted, allowing the sun to have the pleasure of shining its rays through those silken strands, the colour changed to a vibrant gold. Her cheeks were tinged with pink, due more to the freshness of the air than any make-up and her eyes were a dazzling bright blue. Although he now knew she wore contacts, they enhanced her beauty rather than detracting from it.

'Sure. Where's your son?'

'Ah…' Justin looked around the one-acre

paddock Stasy referred to as her back yard. 'Over there.' He pointed to the two boys at the base of the tree that had the tree-house in it.

'Oh, he's with Tim. Good.'

'Which one's Chelsea?' he asked.

Stasy smiled. 'The one wearing the "birthday girl" headband.' Stasy pointed out her not-so-subtle daughter and Justin noted she had similar colouring to her mother.

'You've certainly got a lot of room.'

She chuckled. 'You're not wrong. We like a bit of space and it's very relaxing here.'

'Terrific tree-house.'

'Thanks. My dad built that for the kids a few years before he died. He was a carpenter and helped me to really fix this place up.'

'My mother mentioned that your parents passed away two years ago. That can't have been easy for you.'

'It wasn't but, then, death rarely *is* easy. Anyway, I have Skye.' Stasy pointed out her sister. 'And the twins.'

'Family's vitally important,' he said.

'You've said something like that before.' She looked up at him and it was Wednesday all over again. She was standing close, he could feel her warmth, smell her scent and could drown in her hypnotic eyes.

Justin broke the moment by forcing himself to look away. Why did he seem to get so caught up in this woman's beauty? Every time he was close and could look into those amazing eyes of hers, he felt as though his world melted away and there was only the two of them. It was an odd sensation and one he hadn't felt in years.

He pointed to the tree-house again. 'That really is a beauty. I know Mike was eager to see it. I think it's every kid's dream to have a real cracking tree-house like that.'

'You can go and take a look if you like.'

'Maybe later.' He took a step to the side to put a bit more distance between them, hoping it would help him control the urge to stare into her eyes for a good long while. 'What can I do to help?'

'You obviously don't know Stasy that well,' another woman said, coming over. 'Hi. I'm Skye, Stasy's little sister.'

'Justin. Pleased to meet you.' The two shook hands and Justin couldn't have been more surprised that this woman was Stasy's sister. Where Stasy was blonde and had blue eyes, Skye had dark brown hair with hazel eyes.

'He's got that look on his face, sis,' she remarked.

'What look?'

'The one that says you're trying hard to find the family resemblance. Don't worry about it. Stasy's technically my half-sister. We have different mothers.'

'My mother died when I was only a baby,' Stasy added. 'My dad remarried before I turned two but it took quite some time before Skye was born. At any rate, Skye's mother was my mother in every sense of the word, so it's not something that bothers either of us.'

'Yep, we're sisters all right.' Skye put her arm around Stasy, then eyed Justin carefully. 'Our dad used to say he was a very lucky man as he'd been blessed twice in love.' She put on a deep voice and mimicked her father. 'Just when you think you have your cards all sorted out, you pick up the ace of hearts and suddenly you have a royal flush.' Skye shrugged and resumed her normal tone. 'He liked playing poker.'

'He sounds like a wonderful man.'

'He was,' Stasy said, and decided her little sister had done enough damage for the moment, being as subtle as a sledgehammer with her story. 'Now, did you say you wanted to help?'

'Why did I open my big mouth?' he asked Stasy twenty minutes later as he stood in front of the largest barbecue plate he'd ever seen and turned what appeared to be over two hundred sausages.

'I'm a firm believer in that if people offer to help, give them a job. If they didn't want one, they shouldn't have offered.'

'Touché,' he said with a chuckle. 'I can't believe how many people are here.' Justin swirled the onions around on the corner of the hotplate, the aromas wafting through the air, reminding him that it had been quite some time since he'd last eaten. 'Is this usual for a birthday party in your family?'

'Pretty much. We have the room and this way the kids get to play with all their friends. You'll find most of the boys end up outside and the girls will be inside, trying on clothes and doing their hair and make-up.'

Justin smiled. 'I'm glad I have a son.'

'Girls aren't that bad.'

'I wasn't complaining, just stating a fact. I like girls. Always have.' He waggled his eyebrows up and down as he spoke and again she realised he was flirting with her.

A group of children raced by, laughing and yelling, two dogs barking as they joined in the fun. And, lo and behold, three ducks waddled along behind them. He'd already noticed a

guinea-pig cage and Mike had brought over a
rabbit to show him.

'Are the animals all yours?'

'Yes. Two dogs, two rabbits, two guinea-pigs,
five ducks, three chickens and a partridge in a
pear tree.'

'Really?'

'Well, not the bit about the partridge but it
feels that way sometimes. We also have birds
who come twice a day to be fed.' She pointed
to the bird house which stood over to the left
of one of the lemon gums. 'Sometimes we get
cockatoos but they just make a mess so we try
not to encourage them.'

Stasy picked up a pair of tongs and turned
the sausages before pointing to her left. 'Over
there is my sadly neglected vegetable garden.
Last year I had an amazing crop of carrots
and beetroot. Currently I have some
tomatoes, beetroot, celery and silver-beet
seeds in but the weeds are my best, as you can
see.' She smiled and was rewarded with a

small one from Justin. 'Of course, it's a bit cool for every thing to be out, but I'm looking forward to a good crop when the warmer weather comes.'

'I suppose you bottle your own sauce.'

'Of course, and we pickle our own beetroot, too, but we've run out of that.' She picked up the tomato sauce bottle from the centre of the main table. 'This is from last year's crop.'

Impressed, he nodded. 'I'll have to make sure I try some.'

'You do that.'

'So, tell me, Dr Roberts, when do you find time to actually practise medicine?'

Stasy sighed and smiled up at him. 'Sometimes, Professor Gray, I wonder the same thing myself.'

She shouldn't have smiled up at him. Justin wished she hadn't but she had—and it was such a lovely smile, too. It brightened her face, tilted her eyes up and made their blue depths sparkle with the love of life that radiated from within her.

Something stirred deep in his gut and he tried hard to ignore it but knew it was pointless. Admitting he found Anastasia Roberts attractive was easy enough. Admitting she was beginning to affect him was another.

He'd loved once and he'd lost her to cancer. The intensity of the emotions had ripped him apart and it had taken quite a while before he'd felt remotely able to cope with life again. Now, though, the severity of the feeling of loss wasn't as great and he knew time was healing him.

Loving someone and losing them was tragic and something he'd thought he'd never recover from...but he had. He'd kept on breathing, every day.

'Hello, dear.' Katherine leaned over and hugged Stasy, forcing Justin to look away and to concentrate on his task of cooking the food. 'I've been trying to get over to say hello since we arrived but I've been caught talking to this person and then that one.'

Stasy laughed. 'It's fine, Katherine.' The two women made small talk for a while before Stasy excused herself to go and greet another guest who'd just arrived.

'You like her, don't you?' Katherine said, and Justin looked at his mum in surprise. 'It's all right, you know. It's all right to like another woman, to be intrigued by another woman.'

'Mum!'

'Some people, son, are given second chances. I'm not saying you should forget Rose. You shouldn't. She was a wonderful woman and a great mother but life goes on.'

'I know. Why do you think I'm here? Why we moved from Melbourne? Mike needed more stability.' He turned the sausages, pulling off the cooked ones and putting them on a tray lined with foil to keep them warm.

Katherine placed her hand on his arm and turned him to face her. 'You're doing a good job, son. Your father and I are very proud of you and we've both noticed big differences in Mike since you arrived, but don't just concentrate on Mike. *You* need to move on, darling.'

'And you think Stasy Roberts is the answer?'

'Well, why not? She's beautiful, intelligent and you have medicine in common.'

'Mum. Stop trying to matchmake.' He shook his head. He'd known this would happen, known his mother would take this tack, but he couldn't blame her. He knew she just wanted to see him happy again.

'I won't say anything else except—' Justin laughed '—don't push her away. If there *is* something special between you, embrace it, son. Let yourself be free again.'

They were wise words and he knew his mother wouldn't have dreamed of interfering if she didn't think it was absolutely worth it. He had to admit that since his return to Mount Gambier, since he'd first met Stasy Roberts, he'd begun to feel different. Whether it was the change in physical location, the less demanding job or the fact that Mike seemed to be starting to settle, for the first time in years he had started to think of himself.

What did *he* want?

He was pensive as he took a few more sausages from the barbecue, not sure he knew the answer. The fact that he was even considering moving on was a huge step. He hadn't expected to be attracted to his new colleague but the fact of the matter was—he *was* attracted. It was as simple as that. Whether anything came of it remained to be seen but from the few electrifying moments he'd shared with Stasy, it seemed clear she was as interested as he was. Wasn't she?

As the afternoon progressed, Justin found himself cooking more and more sausages as more and more people arrived. He managed to hand over the cooking duties to police officer Brad and headed over to take a look at the treehouse. Mike, Tim and a few other boys were up there so he had to get permission to come up.

'There are no girls allowed,' Mike sternly told his father.

'Right. Lucky I'm not a girl.' He shook hands with Tim. 'Happy birthday.'

'Thanks.'

'Nine, eh? Getting to be quite the old man.'

'I'm the man of the house,' he declared proudly. 'It's been that way for years. My dad left us when we were babies.'

'Do you ever see him?' Justin asked.

'Nah. He lives in Darwin. He got married again and had some more kids with someone else. He sends us birthday and Christmas cards with money in them. He sent us fifty dollars *each*.'

'Cool,' one of the other boys said.

'Mum said we could either put it in the bank or if we could show her something special we wanted to buy, she'd take us shopping.'

'Cool. What are you going to get?'

The talk turned to computer games and toys and Justin decided it was time he made his exit. Tim seemed very matter-of-fact about his dad. There had been no bitterness in his tone, no concern. He simply seemed to accept that things had turned out the way they had and that was all there was to it. He wondered how it must have been for Stasy, raising two young children alone, trying to fill the gap left by their absent father. She had done so well with them. If only he could do the same in helping Mike fully come to terms with losing his mother.

'If only life were simple,' Justin murmured, and decided to go for a bit of a wander to take in a bit more of Stasy's property. As he rounded the corner of her large shed, he noticed a small hole in the ground with wire around it. 'Sink hole.' He was surprised to find one this far out but then recalled his high-school science lessons about the underground caves that were scattered around this region. Small sink holes weren't so uncommon in Mount Gambier. He skirted the hole and looked out at the view, pleasantly surprised to find the tension of his first week at work starting to slip away in the lush green surroundings.

Stasy watched Justin walk away from the crowds and left him to himself for fifteen minutes before wandering off in the same direction. She found him in the far corner of her property, leaning on the gate that led to the next paddock.

'Had enough of the crowds?' She spoke as she came to stand beside him, leaning forward on the gate next to him. They'd been having quite a wet winter which would hopefully be good news for the summer months as the Blue Lake, which was a dormant volcanic caldera and the town's main water supply, would be nice and full.

'It's very…noisy.'

She laughed. 'How polite of you, Professor.'

'My mother raised me right proper, she did.' Justin's bad Cockney accent made Stasy chuckle before they settled into a companionable silence, both drinking in the view. 'It's a nice place you have here, Anastasia,' he said after a while.

'Thank you. I like it.'

'When did you move here?'

'My husband and I bought it just after we got married. He renovated it but once it was done he wanted to sell it and move on to the next white elephant. That sort of thing.' She shook her head and sighed. 'I couldn't do it. I needed to stay and now I'm glad I did.'

'The kids certainly have enough room to run off their excess energy.'

'One of the many benefits. That's one of the things I love about Mount Gambier. It's home to over twenty-four thousand people yet ten minutes from the inner city...is this.' She spread her arms to indicate the spectacular countryside before them.

'As I said, it certainly is beautiful.'

Again there was a silence between them and she was pleased that it wasn't strained. It seemed odd to be able to just stand there and enjoy a silence with a man she didn't really know. The fact that she *could* do it started the warning bells ringing.

'Oh. I was going to ask you,' she said, suddenly remembering something. 'Tim and Chelsea said their class is studying geology at the moment.'

'There's certainly plenty of it in this area. Caves, sink holes. Limestone is so porous.'

'True. They apparently have to do a project on one of the town's geological tourist sites.'

'Actually, I do remember Mike saying something about it, although he didn't seem too enthused.'

'Oh? He's not into geology?'

'He's not into much of anything. Coming to this party is the most animated I've seen him in a long time so thank you for having it.'

'You're welcome.' Her curiosity was piqued at his words. Had Mike been depressed after his mother's death? It wouldn't be the first time a child had become lost in a world of grief.

'Anyway, Chelsea said most of the class are either doing the Blue Lake or Umpherston's sink hole but my kids have always enjoyed the Tantanoola caves. The area is riddled with stalactites and stalagmites and straws and shawls and all those spectacularly natural decorations. They're allowed to work in teams for the project and I know both the kids were wanting Mike to be in their group.'

'Tantanoola caves? I haven't been there in…wow…such a long, long time.'

'Do you want to take them on Friday after school? We both have the afternoon off,' she said quickly, then shrugged. 'I checked the schedule.'

Justin smiled at that. 'You *drew* up the schedule, you mean.'

She spread her arms wide. 'I did it before I knew about this and, besides, you have the power to change it if you so choose now that you're head of department.'

He nodded. 'Yes, I do. It's a good idea. Let me talk to Mike about it and I'll let you know.'

'Okey-dokey.'

They smiled at each other, neither of them speaking as they just stood there, grinning like a pair of goofy teenagers. The pull, the attraction, the tension she'd experienced before was there again and, as previously, it started doing crazy things to her equilibrium. Justin Gray was knocking her off balance and that was something she wasn't at all used to. Stasy almost willed him to speak, to let her know what he was thinking, but after a whole minute had passed, he turned to look out at the scenery again.

'It *is* beautiful here. The colour is so... vibrant.'

'Mum! Mum!' Tim came hurtling around the corner, narrowly avoiding the small sink hole, his face white with shock. 'Come on. Come *on*!'

'What is it? What's the matter?' she asked as both she and Justin headed back towards the house.

'It's Mike's granddad. He's choking.'

CHAPTER FIVE

'HE CAN'T stop coughing and he's having trouble breathing and no one could find you and Aunty Skye's already rung the ambulance and—'

'It's fine,' she said to her son as Justin raced ahead of her, desperate to help his father. Stasy wasn't far behind, having sent Tim to get her medical bag from the car. Justin came up right behind his father whose body was racked with a spasm. Herb sucked in a breath of air, his eyes widening in terror as he tried once more to breathe. He gasped several times, the sound rasping and filled with fear but still unsuccessful.

'Do something! Do something!' Katherine was pleading. Justin bent his father over the back of a chair and struck him firmly between the shoulder blades, trying to dislodge the obstruction, but it was no good.

'Try to relax,' Stasy said as she took Katherine's hands. 'He'll be fine. We'll make sure of it. Breathe, Katherine. We don't need you passing out as well. Breathe. That's it.' She glanced over to where Justin was still trying to dislodge whatever it was from Herb's windpipe.

'Dad?' Mike's voice was quiet, his eyes wide with shock. 'Grandpa?'

Justin didn't look up, couldn't look up. Mike just stared and watched in mounting horror along with everyone else.

'Here's your bag, Mum,' Tim said, out of breath as he ran towards Stasy. Stasy was taking in the whole scene—Justin, Herb, Katherine, Mike. Seeing how frozen with fear Mike was, she beckoned over Skye, who had been shepherding the other guests into the house, and placed his hand in her sister's. 'Skye, could you take Mike back to the house, please?' Stasy crouched down and patted his shoulder before taking her bag from her son, her voice gentle but firm. 'Your dad and I will take care of your grandpa, Mike, don't you worry. Skye and Tim will stay with you, and we'll come and find you shortly.'

Thankfully he nodded and allowed Skye to draw him away. Despite her words of reassurance, Stasy knew things weren't looking good. Justin was still trying to remove the obstruction but to no avail. Herb was still struggling for breath but at least a tiny bit of air was getting through. By now the muscles in the larynx would be swelling and soon even that tiny bit of air was going to be cut off.

'It won't budge.' Justin's voice was firm and in control as he laid his father down on the ground. 'Dad. Listen to me. This might be a little scary but I'm going to do an emergency tracheostomy.' Stasy saw the pained look in Herb's eyes. 'It's the only way to keep you breathing. You'll be fine. I've done this hundreds of times. Trust me.'

Stasy knelt down on Herb's other side and handed Justin a pair of gloves, then a swab. Justin wiped it over the area where he was about to make the incision. 'I know this sounds silly,' Justin said, 'but try to relax.' He held out his hand for the scalpel and Stasy put it firmly into his palm. There was no need to communicate with words, no need for him to tell her what he needed. She had everything ready and waiting and he was pleased not to have to exert himself any further than he already was. It was true that he'd performed emergency tracheostomies before but never on his father, and it took that extra bit of professional training to push that thought to the back of his mind.

'Oh, dear. Oh, dear. What's he doing?' Katherine was becoming frantic.

'Herb's throat is swelling, Katherine. He can't breathe,' Stasy replied calmly. 'Justin's making a small incision into the trachea—the windpipe—so air can get to Herb's lungs.' She wiped away the blood and handed Justin a piece of tubing she'd prepared.

A gurgling, rasping sound came from Herb as he took a breath.

'Don't try and talk. Just focus on relaxing your body. You're all right,' Justin reassured his father. There was love and respect in his words and it warmed Stasy's heart. Justin was a good man. A caring man. And he'd just saved his father's life.

Justin and Katherine travelled in the ambulance with Herb and Stasy took Mike to the hospital. 'It's my fault,' Mike said quietly in the back of the car.

'What?' Stasy shook her head. 'Why do you say that?'

'I should have stayed with Grandpa. I should have stayed. I shouldn't have gone with my friends. It's my fault. It's all my fault and now Grandpa's going to die and I can't stop it!'

Stasy pulled up at the hospital and cut the

engine. Without a word she climbed into the backseat of the car and put her hands firmly on Mike's shoulders. 'Look at me,' she instructed, and when he did so, she saw the pain in his eyes. It wasn't just his grandpa that was worrying him and she understood Justin's previous comments about wanting to get Mike settled. The boy had already lost his mother and now he thought his grandpa was going to die, too. He needed reassurance and fast.

'This is not your fault. All right? And your grandpa is *not* going to die.'

'But he was so…' Mike broke off, starting to cry. 'Mum looked sick.' He shook his head quickly. 'She tried to hide it with make-up and stuff but she was sick and Dad kept saying she would get better but she never did.' Mike leant against Stasy and she gathered the boy into her arms. 'She left me,' he sobbed. 'She left me.'

Stasy held him, rubbing his back slightly but just holding him, letting him cry. Something told her he'd bottled it up for way too long and now, seeing his grandpa in trouble, it had brought it all to the fore.

Stasy didn't tell him to shush, didn't try to talk to him, to explain things. He just needed to be held and she understood that feeling all too well. It was how she felt some nights—lonely and needing someone around to just hold her, to touch her, to let her know she was cared for. Her heart ached for him and she drew him closer to her.

She brushed away a tear that slid down her own cheek and looked out of the car window just in time to see Justin heading their way. He opened the rear passenger door, his eyes meeting hers.

'Mike? Mike? What is it, mate?'

Justin's words only made Mike cry even more, and cling firmly to Stasy.

'He's releasing,' Stasy said softly, and shifted herself and Mike over so Justin could sit down, with Mike between them. 'How's your dad?'

'I've left Gene to settle him. He'll be fine.'

Justin put his hand on Mike's head, as though he needed to touch his son.

Stasy nodded and continued to rub Mike's back. The sobs were starting to diminish now and she could feel the little body becoming more heavy as he leaned on her. 'My goodness, you're heavy,' she said to him. 'Here, why don't you lean on your dad? He's much stronger than I am.' She shifted slightly and Mike moved with her, turning himself around and allowing himself to be enveloped by his father's strong and protective arms.

Stasy watched as Justin closed his eyes, breathing in the feel, the scent, the need of his son. It touched her heart to see a father so dedicated to his son and she brushed away another tear, wishing her own children could know such a feeling. They'd missed out on their father for almost all of their lives and the mistakes she'd made back then, the ending of her marriage and the fact that it had robbed the children of their father, was something she just had to live with.

Thinking they wanted to be alone, she went to get out but Justin reached for her, catching her hand and stopping her. 'Stay,' was all he said, and went back to holding his son.

Stasy was overwhelmed at being allowed to continue sharing in such a private moment and she knew in that instant that whatever it was that existed between herself and Justin had just escalated.

They sat there for a few more minutes, Mike leaning against his father, hiccuping every now and then, but his breathing was deep and calm. When he lifted his head he looked up at his dad.

'Do you have a tissue?'

Both Justin and Stasy smiled. Justin pulled a handkerchief from his pocket. 'Think this will do?' Mike took the handkerchief and blew his nose. 'Ready to go see how Grandpa's progressing?' Justin asked, and received a mild shrug from his son as an answer. 'He's all right, Mike. He might look a bit funny with a few tubes coming out of him but they're just tubes, mate. Tubes don't stay in for ever and Grandpa *will* get better.'

'Promise?'

'I promise.'

Mike thought on that for a moment. 'You never promised me that Mum would get better.'

'I couldn't, mate. I really wanted to but I couldn't.' Justin ruffled his son's hair.

Mike nodded. 'But you can promise Grandpa will get better from this?'

'I can. It may take a while but he'll be back to talking and chewing his food properly in no time.'

That seemed about enough for Mike at the moment and he leaned across his father and opened the door. They all climbed out and Stasy locked the car before following the Gray men into the hospital. Justin first checked that his father was all right to see Mike and when Herb agreed, they took the boy through.

'See? He's fine. He can't talk,' Justin said, 'but he's fine.'

'You're looking a little better,' Stasy told

Herb. 'A bit of colour back in your cheeks. Good to see.' She picked up the chart from the bottom of his bed and nodded, pleased with the situation. They'd managed to remove the obstruction but Herb would need to have the tubes in until the ENT consultant arrived. 'Excellent progress,' she said, handing the chart to Justin. Gene had removed the makeshift tubes she and Justin had inserted and replaced them with proper tracheostomy tubes. Herb was hooked up to the EEG machine, had the oximeter on his finger and seemed to be surrounded by monitors and leads.

'It may look a little scary at the moment,' Justin said softly to his son as Mike held his grandpa's hand, 'but in a few days things will be better.'

'He won't need to have the tubes all the time?'

'No. This is just temporary.'

Katherine sat on the other side of her husband, holding his other hand, and Stasy put her hand on the woman's shoulder. 'How are you holding up?'

'I'm…holding,' she replied with a sigh. 'I want to stay here tonight.' Her tone was definite. 'Can I do that? Can I sleep beside him?'

Justin looked at Stasy, not sure what the hospital protocols were. 'Of course,' Stasy quickly replied. 'I'll get a private room organised for both of you.' She left the cubicle, giving Justin and his family some time alone, and went to the nurses' station to talk to Gene, who was just getting off the phone.

'That was the ENT consultant. He said he'll be down tomorrow morning to review Herb.'

'Great. Thanks for organising that.' She told him about Katherine's request to stay.

'I'll get that done. You'd best get back to the party.'

Stasy shook her head and sat down in the chair beside him. 'My poor kids. I doubt this is a birthday they'll forget in a hurry.' She smiled as she spoke. 'Why do these things always happen to me?'

'Because you're an emergency specialist?' Gene asked, feigning confusion. 'Hang on. Is this a trick question?'

Stasy laughed and stood. 'I'll go and see what Justin wants to do.'

'We're ready to go,' he said from behind her, and she turned around to see both him and Mike walking towards her.

'You don't want to stay a bit longer?'

'It's fine. Mike and I want some birthday cake, don't we, Mike?'

Mike managed a smile. 'Yeah. Tim told me there were two cakes and his was a big chocolate mud cake and I love that stuff. We used to have cake in Ackland Street in Melbourne with Mum all the time, didn't we Dad? It was really yummy and Tim reckons this cake is even better.'

'Well I guess you'll have to be the judge of that,' Stasy said as she watched Justin's face radiate surprise when Mike started talking about his mother. It made her wonder whether Mike hadn't spoken so animatedly since before his mum's death. Perhaps those tears in the car had been more healing than either of them had realised. 'Tim's never had mud cake from Ackland Street before.'

'You'd better save me a piece,' Gene told Stasy. 'I love your cakes.'

'You made the birthday cakes?' Justin asked Stasy when they'd said goodbye to Gene and headed outside.

'I always do.'

'I had a look at them not long after we arrived. They look amazing.'

'Thanks.' Stasy climbed into the driver's seat and started the engine, waiting to ensure Mike had his seat belt on.

'When did you have the time to make them?'

'Well…who needs sleep?' was her answer.

'You were up all night?'

'It made a nice surprise for the kids when they woke up this morning. Besides, I couldn't sleep.'

'Insomnia, Dr Roberts?'

'Overactive mind, Professor Gray,' she replied. 'I like baking. I find it…relaxes me. Tim's cake was pretty straightforward but Chelsea wanted a cake of a doll wearing a beautiful ballgown, which took a bit more time to put together.'

They continued to talk about the party and cakes and food until they got back to Stasy's house. 'I'm really hungry now,' Justin said.

'Just make sure you chew your food properly, Dad,' Mike said from the back and both adults nodded and smiled at him.

'Good point, son. Thanks for the advice.'

There were so many cars around her property that it was easier to park the car out the front on the road. As soon as she'd cut the engine, Mike jumped out and raced off to see his friends. Justin sat there for a moment and just watched as Mike was joined by Tim and a few other boys before they ran off in the direction of the tree-house.

'He looks different. Older somehow.'

'They do that.' Stasy paused before asking, 'Has he ever cried like that before? About his mum, I mean.'

'No.' Justin turned to look at her. 'No he hasn't. But I'm glad he finally has.' He gave a faint smile. 'I'm only sorry you sort of caught the brunt of it.'

'Justin Gray, don't you dare apologise. I'm honoured I could be there for him, and for you, too, for that matter.'

Justin picked up her hand and held it between both of his. 'I'm glad you were there, too.'

Heat flamed its way through Stasy's body at his touch and she looked down at their hands then back to his face, seeing his heartfelt thanks reflected in his eyes. 'Well, you know…that's what friends are for,' she said hesitantly, forcing herself to speak. The way he was holding her hand, almost cradling it tenderly, was enough to send her unstable emotions into overdrive. He was looking at her in a way no other man had, and she discovered she liked it very much.

'Is that what we are? Friends?' He rubbed his thumb over the back of her hand, caressing gently.

'I g-guess.'

'Your skin is so soft, Anastasia. How do you do it?'

'Do what?' She was mesmerised by the way he was overpowering her senses. Everything seemed to be going haywire. When Justin looked at her, she recognised desire in his eyes and wasn't sure how she should react. Her heartrate was starting to increase, forcing her breathing to follow suit, and she parted her lips, unable to break from his gaze.

'How do you appear to have a hold over me?' His words were barely audible but she heard them.

'Justin,' she whispered, although she wasn't sure why. Did she want him to continue touching her hand? Did she want him to back off? Did she want him to come closer? Stasy's mind began shutting down and instead she decided to let loose, to see where this amazing moment took them. It was risky. It was totally unlike her and that only made matters even more exciting.

When he let go of her hand and raised his fingers to caress her cheek she sighed, trembling at the touch. Her eyelids fluttered closed for a moment and Justin took the opportunity to brush his thumb lightly over the delicate skin. Stasy gasped and quickly opened her eyes to look at him, desperately trying to read his expression, desperately trying to get a handle on the emotions he was evoking.

'Skin so soft,' he murmured, his hand warm but welcome on her cheek. When he tucked a piece of hair behind her ear and then let his hand sift down through the blonde strands, she felt as though she was going to melt into a pool at his feet. 'Your hair is…' He stopped, searching for the right word but slowly shook his head. 'I had a dream last night that I was touching your hair, much like this.'

'You…' The wind rushed out of her lungs at his words and she began to tremble. Swallowing, she tried again, unable to believe what was happening. 'You had a dream about me?'

'I did. I hope that's all right.'

'Ye-yeah.' She moved her head slightly and the warmth from his hand radiated through her once more. She leaned into the touch and sighed.

'Can new friends dream about each other?' he asked. 'I'm not sure how things work any more. Political correctness…' As he spoke, he continued to sift his fingers through her silken strands. 'Always confused me.'

'It's fine. I mean…er…I guess it's OK for two… friends to…' She sighed as he leaned a little closer. 'Justin?' She closed her eyes, savouring everything, committing it to memory.

'Mmm?'

'What is this?' Stasy opened her eyes and looked at him again.

'I don't know.' He tucked her hair behind her

ear once more and shifted in the seat. 'For some reason, though, I can't seem to stop thinking about you.'

'I know.'

'You do?'

'Not that you're thinking about me, I mean… I do *now* because you just told me but I can't seem to stop…thinking about you either.'

'Really?' He straightened his shoulders a little at that news, amazed at how it made him feel.

'We don't know each other. We're new colleagues and…'

'Friends?' he asked when she didn't continue.

'I want to be, but what about this thing? Where is it going to lead?'

'I don't know. You don't know. Perhaps we're not meant to know. Perhaps we're just meant to see where this takes us. Enjoy the journey.'

Stasy shook her head at his words and he dropped his hand. 'I can't do that, Justin. I'm not that sort of person. I like to know where things are heading, to understand them, to make sense of them.'

'It's the scientist in you. I understand but this is also a step out of the ordinary for me, too.'

'That's good to know.'

'Whatever it is, though, we can take it as slowly as you like.'

'Should we be taking…it…anywhere to begin with?'

There was a tap at the car window and Stasy almost hit her head on the roof, she jumped so high. It was Chelsea, and Stasy quickly opened the door and climbed out. 'You scared me.'

'What were you doing? You've been back for ages.'

'Er…Justin and I were…er…talking.'

'We want to cut the cakes, Mum, and everyone keeps asking about Mike's grandpa.'

'You organise the cakes and I'll go give everyone an update,' Justin said as he came to stand beside Stasy.

'Go in to the kitchen and get the paper plates, please,' Stasy instructed her daughter.

'The pink ones?' Chelsea's grin was wide with delight.

'Sure. Whatever.' Stasy really couldn't be bothered with paper plate colour at the moment. 'I'll be there soon.' Chelsea ran off and Stasy turned to look at Justin, aware of his close proximity. He shoved his hands into his jeans pockets and smiled at her.

'Never a dull minute with kids around, eh?'

Stasy returned his smile and nodded. 'You've got that right.' She paused, then pointed to the house. 'I'd better go.'

'Wait a second. Let me just ask you one thing.'

'What?'

'You mentioned that you'd dated in the past.'

'Yes.'

'Did any of the men you dated have children?'

Stasy thought, then shook her head. 'No.'

'None of them?'

'There weren't that many men, Justin. Three—no, four.'

'You've dated four men in eight years?'

'No. I've been on four *dates* in eight years.'

His eyebrows hit his hairline. 'Only one date each?'

'Yes.'

'I'd better watch my step, then.'

'Why? Are you asking me out on a date?'

'I thought you'd already done that.'

'When?'

'Next Friday? Tantanoola caves?'

Stasy smiled. 'That's not a date. That's helping the kids with their homework.'

'But we'd be together.'

'Together with three children.'

'So?'

She watched his face for a moment. 'You're serious.'

'What better way to get to know each other, apart from working together, I mean?'

'To date with three children in tow?'

'They're part of us, Stasy. They've helped make us into who we are.'

She shrugged. 'What do you suggest?'

'How about after we've done the research at the cave, we go out for dinner.'

'The five of us?' She was still astounded with the proposition. When she'd dated in the past, she'd kept the kids well and truly out of it. She'd always thought that if she ever found anyone she wanted to be with, she would first get to know them and then slowly introduce them to the kids. Never had it crossed her mind to actually involve the kids in the dating process.

'Yes.'

'Stalactites and dinner.'

'Yes.'

'Wait a minute. *Where* are we supposed to take them?'

'There are plenty of family restaurants around.'

'I'm not a big fan of junk food.'

'I'm not talking about junk food. Look, leave it to me. I'll take care of it and I promise the food will be healthy.'

She eyed him sceptically.

'Well…relatively healthy,' he amended. 'Now, how about we go and deal with the masses?' He indicated the house which was still filled with party guests. Stasy nodded, knowing, as they both headed towards her back yard, that this was definitely one birthday party she'd *never* forget as it might just be the one that changed her life for ever.

CHAPTER SIX

FOUR days after the party, Justin was able to bring his father home from hospital. Stasy called later that evening to see how Herb was settling in at home.

'He's had some soup and he's all tucked up in bed, watching television,' Justin answered.

'And your mum?'

'She's relieved, I think. It's been really hard on her these last few days but I guess when you know things are only temporary, you cope a little better.'

'And Mike?'

'I think he's happier now that Grandpa is home, too.'

'And you?'

Justin chuckled at her question. 'Checking up on the doctor, eh?'

'Well, you and I both know your father wouldn't have been discharged so quickly if he hadn't been going home with Australia's leading emergency specialist.'

'I doubt I'm that, Anastasia.'

'Why do you do that, Justin? You always put yourself down in a professional capacity. There's no need to. You *are* a brilliant doctor and you *are* considered one of the country's leading experts on emergency medicine. Accept that you're a genius. The rest of us have.'

'It's nice of you to say so but…' He paused. 'I don't know, I feel all pompous and arrogant if I just accept it when people label me.'

'You are *not* pompous and arrogant. Believe me. After marrying a man who had both of those traits, I know them when I see them and you do not have them.'

'You're such an expert, eh?'

'I'm getting to know you more and more every day, Justin.'

'And vice versa.'

'Promise, though, the next time someone says something about your brilliance, just accept it. A polite nod, a smile of thanks. That's all it needs.'

'That's all it needs here in Mount Gambier. It's been great. Now that the staff know who I am and now that I've settled in, I'm not being fawned over. I don't constantly have people asking my opinion on every tiny detail. I don't have a plethora of PhD students requesting me as their supervisor. I don't have to oversee research projects and I don't have to explain or justify every decision I make to a group of colleagues who have me so far up on a pedestal I'm terrified of falling off when they discover I'm a mere mortal.'

'Wow. It was that bad?'

'You once asked if I'd left Melbourne because of stress. I wasn't completely honest with you, Stasy, but it wasn't the pressure of my

job but the pressure put on me by my colleagues to be *perfect*. I'm not perfect. No one
is perfect. Mike was the main reason and you
know that now but, honestly, to go to work at
Limestone Coast every day is a joy and a
pleasure. People are friendly. *Really* friendly,
as though they're interested in me as Justin the
person, not Justin the genius.'

'I guess I'd never thought about it like that
before,' she finally said, unable not to tease
him a little. 'What with me being a mere
mortal an' all.'

Justin chuckled. 'See? You keep me
grounded. You're not afraid to contradict my
opinion or tease me. You're like a breath of
very fresh air, Stasy.'

'And you're a man who's avoiding answering
the real question.'

'What was it again?'

'See? There you go again. I want to know
how *you* are now that your father is home and
out of danger.'

'I'm doing fine, Dr Roberts.'

'Good. I'm not sure I totally believe you but it's enough for now.' She paused, wanting to prolong the conversation but knowing there really wasn't anything left for them to talk about. She racked her brains, searching for a topic, but none came. 'OK, well, I just called to see how everything went with Herb's transfer. Glad it's all under control. I guess I'll see you tomorrow.'

'Stasy, wait.'

She closed her eyes and sent a silent prayer of thanks. 'Yes?'

'I want to thank you for your support these past few days.' He lowered his voice and his words were a little stilted. 'Also, I want you to know it wasn't…easy, seeing my dad like that. He's always been the healthy one. Strong as a Mallee bull. Mum's been the fragile one, with her asthma and so on.'

'Does this mean you're not as fine as you thought?'

Justin took a breath in and exhaled it. 'When I say I'm fine, I mean I'm fine-fine but perhaps not *fine*.'

'Oh, yeah. That makes perfect sense.' Stasy laughed and Justin felt its full effects down the phone line.

'I like the way you laugh.' Justin leaned back in the chair and put his feet up on the sofa, knowing his mother would be cross if she caught him.

Stasy warmed all the way through at his words. 'Hey, don't change the subject.'

'Why not? I don't want to focus on me.'

'Well, you have to. It's my duty as a medical professional to ascertain whether you're of suf-ficiently sound mind and body to be caring for your father.'

'Sound mind and body? I'm not drawing up a will, Stasy.'

She laughed again and he allowed the melody to wash over him. Whenever he'd been with her at work, she'd been almost shy and a little reserved, especially if the two of them had been alone. It brought a sweetness to this burgeoning relationship they'd found themselves in. This was the first time he'd really spoken to her on the phone after hours and he was thoroughly enjoying the flirting.

'Still, I need to know you're going to be all right.'

'I'll be fine.'

'So you've said, and then contradicted yourself and now repeated it, but I'm thinking of letting it slide because I'm also getting confused.'

'You and me both,' he said.

Again there was a pause and Stasy once more tried to think of something to say, something witty and bright to make him smile. She knew he was smiling, could hear it in his words, and, oh, what words he was speaking! Saying that he liked her laugh was like handing her the moon, and no man had ever done that for her before.

'Uh…did you get that file I put on your

desk?' she eventually blurted out, and hit herself in the head. *Way to go, Stase. Real witty.*

'No work, Stasy,' was all Justin said.

'What?'

'I'm not going to talk to you about work. Not now. That can wait until tomorrow. Whatever is happening between us is separate from the hospital.'

'Oh. OK. Uh…well…what do you want to talk about, then?'

'You.'

'That's a boring topic, Justin.'

'I beg to differ. I find you rather…interesting. And just for the record, I was wiggling my eyebrows up and down when I said *interesting,* which means the word was used as a double entendre,' he added, making her laugh.

'You're funnier than I realised.'

'That's good. I think.'

'Oh, it's good all right.'

'You don't laugh much?'

'Nothing to laugh *at* is more to the point.

Until I met you—not that I'm implying I'm laughing *at* you. I meant laughing *with* you. Oh, this is bad.' Stasy hit herself on the forehead again, glad he couldn't see how embarrassed she was.

'See? This is good. This is getting to know each other.'

'It's easier than I thought it would be.'

'To get to know someone?'

'Yes.'

Justin thought for a moment before asking, 'Did he hurt you?'

'Wilt?'

'Is that your ex-husband?'

'Yes.'

'Then I guess that's who I'm asking about.'

'Did he hurt me? Yes. Did he rip my self-confidence to shreds? Yes. Did he make me doubt my natural feminine ability? Yes. Was his leaving a good thing? Yes.'

'What happened?'

'Nothing dramatic. He didn't run off and

have a torrid affair. We just had different ideals about how our life should turn out. Wilt's a builder and wanted to move around the country. I wanted to stay in one place and work, raise a family. My dad was in the armed forces so we moved quite a bit when I was growing up and I was more than happy to stay in one place when I finally started university in Adelaide. When my parents retired to Mount Gambier, well, it seemed the right place to come and practise medicine.'

'So when Wilt wanted to move around?'

'That's when the arguing started. We'd been married for three years when I became pregnant with the twins. He was gone two weeks before our fifth wedding anniversary.'

'Where is he now?'

'Uh…let me check the postmark on the cards he sent to the kids. I think it's Darwin.' She hunted around for a few seconds. 'Yes. Darwin was where they were posted. There's no return address, there never has been.'

'He pays child support, though, right?'

'No.'

'He should.'

'I don't want it. My life is happier without him. Lonelier but happier. Not that I'm saying I'm lonely without him.'

'It's all right. I know what you mean.'

'Also, the loneliness is only at certain times,' she clarified. 'Skye and the kids fill a lot of gaps.'

Justin listened to what she was saying and could quite easily read between the lines. The loneliness he'd experienced after Rose's death had surprised him. Try as he might to fill his days with work and his nights with looking after Mike, the loneliness had still engulfed him. Now, though, things were getting easier. He was becoming more comfortable simply being by himself and doing what he chose to do.

'What about you?'

'Meaning?'

'Have you been lonely since your wife died?'

'Of course.'

'But you've found a way to deal with it?'

'I guess I have.'

'How?'

'I chat to colleagues on the phone when everyone's tucked up safe and sound.'

Stasy chuckled. 'Oh, so that's what I've been doing wrong all these years.'

'Exactly. So any time you're feeling lonely, just pick up the phone.'

'What if you're asleep?'

'I'm a doctor. I can wake up instantly.'

'I wouldn't want the phone to disturb anyone else in the house.'

'I sleep with it by my bed and am very quick at answering. In fact, I'll have you know that in medical school we used to have phone-answering competitions and I was the champion.'

Stasy pulled the phone away from her ear for a moment, looked at it as though she thought Justin had gone around the twist before she asked, 'You had *what* competitions?'

'Phone answering. You know, someone would make a pretend ringing sound and the person who answered the phone the fastest would win.'

'You're kidding me?'

'Would I joke about a conquest like that? They didn't call me Quick Draw Gray for nothing.'

'Quick Draw Gray. Now I've heard it all.' Stasy laughed over his words.

'I like the way you laugh.'

'So you've said.'

'I like a lot of things about you, Stasy.'

'The feeling's mutual, Justin.'

'Do we need to hang up now?'

She sighed. 'I suppose we should but I don't really want to.'

'Neither do I.'

'This has been nice.'

'It has.'

'But I do have dreaded paperwork to do before tomorrow.'

'All work and no play makes Stasy a very dull girl.'

'All play and no work makes Quick Draw Professor mad tomorrow when he doesn't get the completed forms he needs to take to the board meeting.'

'Good point.' Justin sat up. 'You know, I do think it's a wise idea for you to continue checking on me to make sure I'm of sound mind and body to continue caring for my father.'

'I take it that means you want me to call you more often?'

'It does.'

'Or you could call me and volunteer an update.'

'I could. I could do that.' He glanced at the clock. 'Speaking of which, I'd better go and check on my dad. Make sure he's brushed his teeth and been to the toilet.'

Stasy smiled. 'You go do that. Perhaps they'll put you in the Son of the Year competition and you can gain a new title.'

He laughed at that and Stasy locked away the memory, knowing she'd need it later when she lay in bed, thinking of him. 'Goodnight, Anastasia.'

'Goodnight, Justin.' Slowly she put the phone down and sat staring out into nothingness for a few minutes, her mind replaying the conversation they'd just had over and over in her head. Of course, she pressed 'pause' and 'replay' at all the best bits. Justin liked the way she laughed. That was such a nice thing for him to have said. She couldn't remember laughing so much with Wilt. Maybe they had in the beginning but she couldn't access those memories, so now she began to wonder if they ever had.

Wilt hadn't flirted with her much either, even when they'd first met and started dating. Justin had spent almost the entire phone call not only showing a real interest in her but flirting as well, and she'd loved every minute of it. At work she was trying to keep things as professional as possible and she was glad he seemed to feel the same way. Whatever it was that existed between them could have dire consequences if things didn't work out. She'd always been a cautious child and now she was a cautious adult. She'd relied on that many a time but with Justin she was also wondering whether stepping up to the plate and taking a chance was the right thing to do.

She could get hurt and not only her. They both had children to think of and their working life would probably end with polite but stilted words, the two of them only speaking when it was absolutely necessary. She'd seen it happen to other couples who'd worked together after a break-up and honestly didn't know what to do. Should she just enjoy the moment? Enjoy the way Justin was making her feel right now? Or should she pull back and put a bit more distance between them?

For the next couple of days at work she kept everything strictly professional. Not impersonal but professional, treating Justin as she did her other colleagues. In the evenings, once the kids were settled in bed and Skye was off studying in her room, she'd call Justin and they'd talk, finding they shared quite a number of common interests. They didn't talk about work on the phone and they didn't talk about the phone calls at work. It was a strange situation but for the moment it was working... whatever *it* was.

Finally Friday afternoon came around and Stasy picked three excited kids up from school, all of them eager to head out to Tantanoola caves to start their researching.

'Where's Dad?' Mike asked.

'Still at the hospital. Sorry. We got waylaid so I'm here to do a quick pick-up and then we're back to the hospital.'

'How long will you be?' Chelsea asked.

'Hopefully not too long. Go to my office and put a DVD on. We'll come and get you when we're ready.'

'All right.' The three children happily traipsed off and Stasy noticed they were becoming as thick as thieves. It was good to see, especially for Mike's sake. Justin had told her the previous night that Mike was starting to talk more openly about his mother and each time he did, each time he realised it was all right to remember his mother, he seemed to become more like his old self. He also spent time before and after school with his grandpa, and that, too, was helping to alleviate any feelings of concern the boy might have.

Today, though, was a special day and the children weren't the only ones who were eager to get the outing under way. Justin had said this would be their first official date so she'd dressed appropriately in a pair of dressy denim jeans, her flat leather boots, which would be perfect for walking around the show cave, and a royal blue sweater. She had her leather jacket with her in case the evening became too cold. She'd decided on her blue contact lenses and was planning to take her hair out of its usual ponytail once they left the hospital, knowing how much Justin liked it loose.

It was strange, choosing her clothes and how to wear her hair with a man in mind. She wanted to look nice for him but was also determined not to be too overdressed. Luckily, the children had had a casual clothes day at school so none of them needed to get changed out of school uniform.

She headed off to A and E to see how Justin was getting on with the patient she'd left him attending to, only to find him sitting at the nurses' station, writing up the notes.

'All done?' she asked.

'Pretty much.' He, too, was dressed more casually today, wearing jeans, walking boots and an open-collared shirt. Of course, their attire had caused both Gene and Christine to make remarks, leaving Stasy with no option but to confess their after-work plans.

'OK, then. I've sent the kids off to my office but I'll go and get them.' No sooner were the words out of her mouth than the doors to A and E swished open and a young mother came in, her face tear-stained as she carried a young baby in her arms.

'Help me,' she said, her voice breaking.

Stasy and Justin were immediately on their feet, one of the nurses in tow. 'Come in here,' Stasy said, and pulled back the curtain to cubicle one. 'What's the problem?'

'He's vomiting. He just keeps vomiting.'

'Reflux?' Stasy questioned.

'Well, that's what my local doctor said but it doesn't matter what I give him or what I do, he still can't keep anything down. I'm getting worried.'

The baby was wailing loudly, making his presence and his pain known to all and sundry.

'What's his name?'

'Jimmy. Jimmy Percival. I'm Tamora.'

'And how old is little Jimmy?' Justin asked the question, raising his voice above the noise.

'Three months.'

'Born here?' Stasy asked as she held out her hands for the child. 'May I?'

'Uh, sure, and, yes, he was born here.'

'I'll get the notes,' the nurse said as Stasy took Jimmy from his mother.

'When was the last time he vomited?' Justin asked, noting how naturally Stasy held the child. Well, having raised twins, he could hardly expect her to be a novice when it came to dealing with babies. She was also holding the baby in a way that she could keep his arms and legs from flailing around long enough for Justin to feel his tummy.

'About ten minutes ago. It scared me because it went all the way across the room. It was like something from a horror movie.' Tamora shuddered.

'Projectile vomiting.' Justin nodded.

'So he has problems settling when it's feed time?'

'Yes. I'm trying to breastfeed him but when I told my doctor that Jimmy wasn't settling, he

said to try him on a bottle. I've tried express-
ing milk. I've tried formula. It's just so hard to
get him to drink.'

'And when he does, he simply brings it all
back up? Over himself and over you?' Stasy
asked with a small smile.

'Yes.'

She nodded. 'My son was like that. Perhaps
not as bad as little Jimmy here, but I do know
what you're going through.' Her words seemed
to calm Tamora's nerves a bit more and again
Justin was impressed with the way Stasy
seemed to know what to say to calm people
down. It was a real gift. 'Dr Gray and I both
have children so we do sympathise.'

'Thanks.'

'Why don't you sit down on the bed,
Tamora?' Stasy suggested as Justin finished his
examination. She started to pace up and down
in the small space, patting little Jimmy's
bottom, hoping to get him to quieten down.
'You must be tired,' she said to the mother.

'I am.' Tamora sighed with relief as she sank onto the bed. 'My husband's away at the moment. In Adelaide. He has to travel for his job but he'll be home tonight.'

'Good.'

'Mrs Percival,' Justin said, 'I'd say young Jimmy here is having more problems than just reflux.'

'Oh?' Tamora's eyes became wide and worried once more.

'There's a congenital defect—that means he was born this way—of his pylorus. The pylorus is the part where the small intestine, or the duodenum, and the stomach meet. Pyloric stenosis, which is what young Jimmy has, is when the pylorus has narrowed and isn't letting food flow properly into the duodenum. It's easy to feel if you know what you're looking for but we'll run more tests to confirm the diagnosis.'

'So…it's not me?' Tamora was surprised.

Stasy shook her head as Jimmy's cries began to settle a bit. 'No. You haven't done anything wrong.' Her tone was intent and imploring. 'You're a good mother.'

Tamora couldn't help keeping the relief from her face. 'Oh, thank goodness. I kept thinking it was me. That I was feeding him wrong or doing something wrong or not doing something.'

'I know. Those first few months you can really beat yourself up if the baby isn't behaving exactly as the books say.'

'The only way to fix Jimmy's problem is with surgery,' Justin continued.

Tamora's face paled. 'Surgery!'

'Yes, but it's a very small operation where the surgeon will widen the pylorus, allowing a clear passage for the food to travel down. It doesn't take long and once it's done, Jimmy will be as right as rain. I'll contact the paediatric surgeon, who is in town at the moment, so he can come and examine Jimmy. He'll discuss the operation with you in more detail, do more tests and hopefully if the emergency operating lists aren't too full, he'll be able to do the operation either this afternoon or early tomorrow morning.'

'As soon as that? Do I get time to think about it?'

'Of course,' Stasy assured her. 'The fact does remain, though, that Jimmy will require an operation to fix this problem but once that's done, he'll be fine.'

'Is this sort of thing common?' Tamora asked Justin.

'It is. I've seen plenty of cases of this in my time.'

Jimmy was starting to settle a bit more and Stasy handed him back to his mother, who was now lying back on the bed. 'Why don't you try and have a snooze while we track down the surgeon? I'll get a crib brought in for Jimmy.'

'No. It's all right. I'll just hold him for now,' Tamora said quickly, hugging her baby close as though to protect him from everything in the world.

'Of course.' Jimmy was only snuffling now, his eyes closed, his breathing starting to return to normal. 'Poor love,' Stasy said, and brushed her hand across his soft, downy head.

Stasy and Justin returned to the nurses' desk and she put in the call to the surgeon, passing on the details.

'Right. Let's get out of here before another emergency comes our way and totally blows our plans out of the water,' Justin remarked.

'Wouldn't be the first time it's happened,' she said, quickly finishing writing up the notes.

'Or the last.' Justin held out his hand to Stasy and she automatically took it, letting him help her up. He didn't drop her hand, as she'd thought he would, and instead held it firmly as they walked up the corridor towards their offices. He didn't let go while they organised their children. Mike noticed first.

'Why are you holding Stasy's hand, Dad?' At his words, all three children looked.

'So she doesn't get lost,' was Justin's reply.

'Come on. Let's get going.' At that, the children all raced out of the office and down the corridor. Justin flicked the lock on Stasy's office door and closed it tight before starting towards the front door.

'Justin. You can let go now,' she murmured, not wanting to cause a scene but completely conscious of a few of the looks they were getting from their colleagues.

'No, I can't.'

'Why not?'

'Because we're on a date.'

CHAPTER SEVEN

THE children were all highly animated as they drove to Tantanoola in Justin's car, leaving Stasy's at the hospital. When they arrived, Stasy handed jackets to all of the children, knowing the temperature would be cool inside the small caves. Justin headed off to investigate as Stasy finished organising the kids. They were armed with the questions they needed to cover for their school project and bubbling with excitement, they waited impatiently for their tour to begin.

Stasy headed over to where Justin was talking with the female guide. She noticed how the other woman smiled brightly at Justin, fluttered her eyelashes and laughed at something he said. Stasy felt a burning in the pit of her stomach. The realisation hit her with full force as she recognised the emotion she was feeling was jealousy. Pure and simple. *She* was here with Justin and she didn't like it one bit that another woman was smiling at him.

She was a gratified, however, that as soon as Justin saw her walking towards him, he immediately broke off and came over to her side, showing he wasn't at all interested in the petite brunette.

'How much is admission?' Stasy asked.

'Don't worry about it. I bought a family pass.'

'F-family?' Stasy only then realised how their little group might be misconstrued. One man, one woman and three children. They *looked* like a family and she realised that it didn't seem to bother Justin at all. That was a good thing, right?

As they began their tour of the cave, which was filled to the brim with amazing natural wonders, they learned that it had only been discovered in 1930 by a local boy, hunting rabbits. The cave structure was mainly dolomite rather than limestone and boasted a large number of helictites. The children wrote the information down and Stasy's feelings towards the guide improved somewhat as she patiently spelt out the different names for the things and made sure the children had a firm understanding of how the speleotherms were created.

'All the cave decorations are calcite from the water coming through the limestone, evaporating in the cavern and leaving the deposits that we see here. And with all this rain,' the guide said with enthusiasm, 'there will be new caves being created and we may even get a sink hole or two forming.'

'Wow!' Chelsea was amazed.

'Engelbrect cave in Mount Gambier may even flood. That's where divers come from all around the world to swim in the underground caves beneath the city.'

'Wow!' Mike was impressed. 'There are caves filled with water beneath the city!'

'Yeah.' Tim nodded enthusiastically. 'It's

totally cool. I want to learn to dive when I'm bigger just so I can go and swim under the city.'

'I'm gonna do that, too,' Mike agreed. Both of them looked expectantly at Chelsea.

'What? I'm not. I think you're both mad.'

'You can have a pink diving suit,' Tim promised.

'Really. Well, in that case, count me in!'

Stasy and Justin couldn't help but laugh at their children as the guide once more told them some new and exciting bit of information.

'Nothing like the incentive of a pink diving suit to get a woman focused, eh?' Justin couldn't resist teasing quietly. Stasy watched as he interacted with all three children, giving Chelsea and Tim as much attention as he did Mike, and was thoroughly pleased with the way the twins responded to him without reservation. Once they'd looked at all the delights of the cave, taking photographs and exclaiming over the underground pool which the kids thought was amazing, they headed back out.

'Thank you,' Stasy said to the guide, now feeling ashamed of her jealous thoughts earlier.

'My pleasure. Let me know if the kids have any more questions. They can call me or definitely come back for another visit any time.'

'We'll keep that in mind,' she said, and offered her hand to the guide.

'You're welcome, Mrs Gray.'

Stasy immediately looked over at Justin, only to find him smiling broadly as they headed back to the car.

'She thought we were married,' Stasy said in a whisper, hoping the kids wouldn't hear her.

'Who thought who was married?' Chelsea asked, slipping her hand into her mother's.

'Nothing, big ears.' Stasy tried to brush it off.

'The guide. She thought we were all one big happy family,' Justin said, half speaking over Stasy's words.

'Really?' Chelsea was surprised for a

moment, then laughed. 'That's too funny. Hey, boys,' she said, and raced ahead to speak to them.

'Now look what you've done.' Stasy wasn't at all sure about this turn of events.

'What?' Justin shrugged. 'It's all right.' He took Stasy's hand in his and brought it to his lips before letting it go. 'Relax. We're on a date, remember. Let's just kick back and have some fun and not care about what some cave tour guide in Tantanoola thinks.' He unlocked the car and the children clambered into the back.

'Justin.' She was trying to keep her brain working, to keep it thinking clearly but he'd just kissed her hand and she was having difficulty keeping her breathing under control.

'Stasy,' he returned, and opened the passenger door for her. They were close again. Almost standing side by side, the door between them. When she didn't speak, when she just stood there looking at him as though she was confused, bewildered and excited all at the same time, he couldn't resist and leaned forward and placed a quick kiss on her cheek. 'Let your mind go, Stasy. Relax. Enjoy yourself. Be free.'

She looked deeply into his eyes and knew that if she really did let go, if she started to enjoy herself and relax, she'd be in grave danger of falling in love with him, and that wasn't what she wanted. Was it?

'I don't know how.' Her words were barely above a whisper but she knew Justin had heard.

'I'll help you.' He smiled that gorgeous smile of his and a wave of reassurance washed over her. It was enough…for now. Stasy climbed into the car and Justin shut her door before coming around to the driver's side.

'Now,' he said to the children after he'd put on his seat belt and started the engine, 'because you've all been so good, with lovely manners towards the guide, as a treat we would like to take you all out to dinner. What do you say?'

'Yay!' All three children cheered. As Justin

drove back to Mount Gambier it was getting near dusk, and even though the road was a dual-carriage highway, they all still watched for kangaroos and other wildlife which might have been out at that time of night.

The kids sang a song they'd learnt at school and generally chatted, none of them showing signs of wearying, so that when Justin finally pulled up in the restaurant car park, the three of them tumbled out, eager for their special evening treat.

'I have to admit,' Stasy said an hour later after the children had eaten quite a bit of food from the large smorgasbord on offer, 'you picked a very good restaurant. I had no idea there was so much here for the children to eat.' The restaurant also had a kids' video game section and all three had gone off to play so she and Justin could talk in peace.

'You've never been here before?'

'No. I've heard of it, of course, but we rarely dine out. Skye's been here, though.'

'Quite an interesting girl, your sister.'

Stasy's smile was natural. 'She's certainly that.'

'When does she finish her studies?'

'Four months—or it might be three months and three weeks. Not sure but the countdown is definitely on.'

'And then?'

'And then she'll leave Mount Gambier and go overseas to work. She's already been offered a position in England to do her doctorate.'

'Impressive.'

'We're all very proud of Skye.'

'I take it she helps out with the kids?'

'She does. She's the best.' Stasy sighed heavily. 'I have no idea what I'm going to do when she goes.'

'You'll cope.'

'I suspect I will.'

'Of course you will,' he said with more enthusiasm. 'You're a survivor, Stasy Roberts.'

'Takes one to know one,' she returned, beginning to feel self-conscious again.

'Why do you do that?' Justin eased back in his chair and looked at her with interest.

'Do what?'

'Whenever I try to pay you a compliment, you try to hide it by turning the tables back onto me.'

'Do I? Sorry. Although you're one to talk, my brainy professor!'

'True. Anyway, I guess I'm a little more than curious as to why you do that. Didn't your husband ever pay you compliments? Tell you how pretty you looked? How he liked a particular piece of clothing?' Justin shifted, leaning forward and placed his elbows on the table, resting his head on his hands. 'Or how your scent manages to make a man forget everything else?'

Stasy was equally as mesmerised by him and came closer but not too close.

'You've hit me for six, Stasy.' His words were intimate but clear. He didn't want any misunderstanding about what he was going to say. There would be no confusion between them.

He wanted her to know he was interested in her and he was interested big time.

'This attraction between us,' he continued. 'It was the very last thing on my mind and I want you to know I'm as confused by it as you appear to be.' He waited for her small nod of agreement before continuing. 'I didn't come to Mount Gambier to have my personal life turned inside out and upside down but that's what seems to be happening. *You* seem to be happening and I don't want to stop it.' He straightened up a little but it was only to reach over and take her hand in his.

'You've made me feel alive again, Stasy, and I never, in my wildest dreams, thought I'd ever feel that way again after Rose died.'

Stasy opened her mouth to speak, to respond to him, but his words had had such a powerful effect on her she discovered she was incapable of speech. She closed her mouth, hoping she wasn't doing her stunned-goldfish impression again.

'I know this may seem sudden and out of the

ordinary and all that but we owe it to ourselves to see where this might lead.'

It was what every woman might want to hear from the man she couldn't stop dreaming about. The man she looked forward to seeing every day. The man who was becoming as important to her as he was telling her she was to him.

'What if it leads to disaster?' she asked, fear and uncertainty evident in her voice.

'What if it doesn't?' he counteracted. 'Look, I'm not saying we need to decide anything right now. We don't.'

'Then what *are* you saying, Justin?'

'I'm saying…I'm *asking* for permission, I guess, to officially date you. We can take things as slowly as you like, let the children get used to the idea—'

'No.'

Justin frowned for a moment before asking carefully, 'No to everything?'

'No. No to the children getting used to us

dating, of us…perhaps…being together. They need stability in their lives and I've worked hard to not only give them that but to maintain it.'

'You can't maintain it for ever, Stasy. I mean, Skye is going to leave soon and their worlds will change, but they're nine years old now. There are things they can do, things they can understand and comprehend now that they wouldn't have been able to do even a few years ago.'

'Justin. I need to protect them.'

'Yes, you do. You're their mother and you do an excellent job, but you must know you can't protect them from everything.'

'Perhaps not, but there are some things that aren't beyond my control and on that score I'd rather play the over-protective parent and make sure they're *not* emotionally hurt in any way, shape or form.'

'So you don't have a problem with the two of us getting to know each other better. Dating.'

'No.'

He frowned in total confusion. 'No, you don't want to or, no, you don't have a problem with it?'

'I want to get to know you, Justin. That much I'm certain of but wc do need to take things slowly...*very* slowly.'

Justin's grin was one of total happiness at that moment. 'We will. I promise. And for now we won't say anything official to the children that we're going to date. How's that?'

'That's good.'

'How about our colleagues? Can they know we're dating?'

'Well, after the way you walked out of the hospital holding my hand, there's a fair-to-sure chance the gossips have started already.'

'Good.'

'Good?'

'Well...uh...don't look now but Cliff and his very pregnant wife are headed in our direction.'

Stasy had but a moment to compose herself before Alison and Cliff appeared by their table.

'I thought it was you,' Cliff said, offering his hand to Justin. 'Stasy. Good to see you.' He looked around. 'You two here alone?'

Justin grinned. 'Alone? How could we possibly be alone when we have three children between us?' He pointed to the games parlour where they could see the kids playing the video games.

'They're doing school projects on geology so we've just got back from Tantanoola caves,' Stasy said, wanting to explain.

'Right.' Alison nodded as though she didn't believe her. 'And that's why you're holding Justin's hand?' she teased.

Stasy's eyes widened in alarm and she quickly looked to check Alison was correct only to find she was. She withdrew her hand.

'Well…uh…we were…uh…'

'Here. Come and sit down,' Justin said to Alison, standing up to offer his own chair.

'I don't know if I can at the moment.' She rubbed her swollen belly. 'I think I ate something junior didn't like.'

Stasy glanced at Justin at the same moment he looked at her, both of them instantly alert to Alison's words. The majority of pregnant women were more than happy to be off their feet as much as possible and if Alison had just finished eating, there was no way the food could have affected her so quickly as to give her indigestion.

'Are the pains sharp?' Stasy asked.

'A little. Just down here.' Alison rubbed the spot.

'Have you been having them long?' Justin asked.

'I've been having them for about two days now.'

'What?' Cliff was surprised. 'Why didn't you tell me?' He instantly placed his hand on his unborn child. 'Where? Are you having a pain now?'

'Is it a contraction or a pain?' Stasy quizzed.

'Uh…I don't know what a contraction feels like. This is my first child. My doctor told me I'd experience Braxton-Hicks' contractions and so it might just be them. Three of my friends have had false calls and been sent home. The way they described feeling is how I'm feeling now…' She stopped talking for a moment as a pain gripped her. Cliff moved his hand around to try and feel the contraction. 'Although they seem to be getting stronger.'

'I think we'll get you to the hospital, my darling.'

'Cliff. I'm fine.' Alison laughed at all three of them. 'I'm fine. Look at you all. You look like over-anxious doctors. Stop fussing. I'm fine.'

'So you keep saying,' Stasy remarked, the memory of the twins' birth flashing before her eyes. 'The fact that you can't sit down, that you've been having these mini-contractions for a few days…Alison, you're in labour.'

'But my water's haven't—' She stopped as she spoke, her expression changing to one of wide-eyed disbelief.

'Broken?' Stasy finished for her and stood, picking up her handbag and taking Alison's hand, leading her carefully to the ladies' room. 'Get the kids,' she called to Justin over her shoulder. 'Cliff, bring the car around and call her obstetrician.'

Alison groaned and held her breath for a moment before letting it go. 'The pains are getting stronger. So quickly, too.'

'You're in labour,' Stasy reiterated as she helped Alison to sort herself out, making her more comfortable for the ride to the hospital.

'Are you sure? I don't want to be sent home from hospital if it's not the real thing. My friends were devastated that they'd got it wrong.'

'It's quite common for first-time mothers to mistake Braxton-Hicks' for labour but these are not Braxton-Hicks', Alison. Add to that fact that your waters have broken and it's better for both you and the baby if you're in a sterile environment.'

'It's probably also better for Cliff. He worries so much. I never knew doctors could worry that much.'

Stasy smiled. 'In this instance Cliff isn't a doctor, he's a husband and expectant father. You've both been through so much to get to this point in your lives. It's too precious to trifle with.'

When they came out of the ladies' room, the men were ready and waiting.

'Come in our car, Stasy.' Alison held her hand tightly. 'I'll feel more relaxed if you're there.'

'Sure.' Stasy nodded and Justin came up behind her, placing his hand on her shoulder.

'We'll drive behind you. If things…escalate, get Cliff to pull over. I have my medical bag in the back of the car.'

'Right. Thanks.' As she spoke, Alison had another contraction. Stasy consulted her watch. 'Three minutes apart. We'd better get moving.'

Thankfully, the drive to the hospital was uneventful in that they didn't need to stop and Alison's contractions remained at three minutes apart. When they arrived, they wheeled her into A and E, and Stasy pulled on a protective gown and a pair of gloves. She'd left Justin to get the kids settled and was astonished at how much she trusted him with her precious children. She was so fiercely protective of them and usually only left them in Skye's care when she was busy at the hospital. Now she was relying on Justin and had no qualms that he'd make sure they were safe and secure in one of their offices. Didn't that tell her how important he was becoming to her?

When she performed an internal examination it was to find Alison was fully dilated and the baby's head beginning to crown.

'How are things?' Justin asked as he entered the room and Stasy crossed to his side.

'We're on duty…at least until Barbara gets here.'

'I take it Barbara's her obstetrician?'

'You take it correctly,' Stasy remarked as she headed back over to Alison. Justin and Stasy worked together, forcing Cliff to simply be there for his wife and to enjoy the experience of the birth of his first child.

By the time Barbara arrived, the head was out and Stasy had checked to ensure the cord wasn't around the baby's neck which, thankfully, it wasn't.

'We're just waiting for the shoulders to rotate,' she told Barbara. 'Alison is doing a brilliant job.'

Both she and Justin stepped back to allow Barbara to take over but they didn't leave. They were a part of this family scenario now and both Alison and Cliff wanted them to stay.

'Did you plan to have more children?' Justin asked Stasy quietly as they stood in the corner and waited. Justin was so close to her, his arm was on the wall behind her and his body was leaning in her direction…and it was nice. It was comforting and secure and she couldn't believe how his nearness made her feel protected.

'You mean if my marriage hadn't come apart at the seams?' She smiled up at him, not at all put out that he'd asked.

'Yes.'

'I'm not sure. I hadn't expected to have twins

first off and I'd really only planned on two.' She shrugged. 'How about you?'

Justin looked down at her and she noticed his eyes grow sad for a moment. 'Rose wanted to have a whole brood. At least six, she used to say. I kept telling her it was just as well I had a good job to pay for them all.' His smile was nostalgic. 'We discovered the cancer when Mike was two and a half.'

'Really?'

'He was too young to understand anything. They removed the primary and she started chemotherapy.' His words were soft and far away. 'We started trying again when Mike was about four and that's when we learned that secondaries had started to appear.'

'Oh, Justin.' Stasy reached up and caressed his cheek. 'I'm so sorry.'

He shifted, leaning into her hand for a moment before she dropped it back to her side. 'Now, when I talk about it, it's as though I'm telling you someone else's story, rather than my own.'

'You've moved on.'

'I don't know when. It's just sort of… happened.' He stared into her eyes, both of them feeling safe and secure with the other for that one moment.

A loud wailing cry pierced the air and both Justin and Stasy snapped out of their bubble in time to see Barbara holding up a very put-out baby girl.

'She was nice and warm inside,' Barbara was saying to the two new parents. 'Let's get her nice and warm out here.'

Justin and Stasy smiled as Cliff clamped and cut the cord before wrapping his daughter in a warmed towel, cradling her tenderly in his arms and showing her to Alison.

'Congratulations,' Stasy said, wiping a tear from her eye.

'Well done. Both of you,' Justin agreed.

'We're going to leave you alone now to bond as a family while we get our respective families into bed, but I'll come by tomorrow to have a proper cuddle with…' She paused. 'Oh, what's her name going to be?'

'Stephanie Anne,' Cliff and Alison said in unison, then smiled at each other.

'Lovely,' Stasy replied, but knew they were past hearing anyone else.

After they'd collected the kids and walked out to the hospital car park, Stasy headed over to her car. 'Thanks for a lovely time, Justin. It was…' She sighed. 'It was the best evening I've had in a very long time.'

'I'm glad to hear that.'

'Mum?' Tim piped up. 'Can Mike come for a sleepover?'

'What?' Stasy was surprised.

'Aw, come on, Mum. It's Friday night, we don't have school tomorrow,' Tim persisted.

'But he doesn't have a change of clothes or a toothbrush,' Stasy pointed out.

'He can borrow some of my clothes,' Tim said eagerly.

'And I haven't opened my new toothbrush

yet,' Chelsea chimed in, then turned to Mike. 'It's purple, though.'

Stasy looked at Justin, unsure what to do.

'Mike, do you want to go for a sleepover?' Justin asked.

'Yeah! That'd be awesome and we could talk some more about our project. We're thinking of making a cave out of paper and cardboard and stuff and then painting it to show all the different types of spelothings.'

Stasy smiled. 'Speleotherms.'

'We can start working on it in the morning.'

Justin shrugged. 'Looks as though they have it all organised.'

'Yay!' the three of them cheered and before either parent could say anything more, they climbed into the back of Stasy's car.

'You don't mind?' she asked.

Justin smiled, 'No. It's great to see. It's another indication that Mike's ready to take the next step, to regain a bit of his independence.'

'When they move, they move fast,' Stasy pointed out, and Justin laughed.

'That they do. It's fine for him to go with you if he's comfortable with it and, of course, if it's OK with you.'

'It's fine. Tim has bunk-beds in his room so there's no great difficulty.'

'Besides all of that, I get to see you in the morning when I come to pick him up.'

'Ah…so that's your grand scheme.'

'I like seeing you, Stasy.' He sifted his fingers through her hair then tucked it behind her ear before bending to kiss her cheek. 'I like spending time with you.'

She closed her eyes at the warm touch, drinking him in, wanting more but conscious they had three children watching them and goodness knew how many patients peering out their windows into the night.

'Slowly,' Justin whispered in her ear and she nodded. When he drew back he smiled down at her. 'We'll take it slowly, Stasy.' He caressed her cheek where he'd just pressed his lips. 'I'll see you for breakfast, Dr Roberts.' He dropped his hand, took two steps away and shoved his hands into his jeans pockets. 'Pancakes. Yes, definitely pancakes.'

'Ready to trust my cooking?'

'If you make pancakes the way you make cakes, I can see me putting on a bit of extra weight.' He patted his flat, firm stomach.

Stasy chuckled and watched as he said good-night to his son. She walked around to the drivers' side and opened the door.

'Drive safely,' he said.

'I will.'

'I'll see you in the morning.'

'Yes.'

He came forward again and kissed her cheek, lingering longer than last time. 'Dream of me,' he whispered.

'Oh, yes,' she breathed on a sigh, and couldn't

believe the feelings of loss that seemed to swamp her as she watched him walk to his car, get in and drive away.

CHAPTER EIGHT

SATURDAY morning dawned brightly and Justin headed out to the kitchen to find his mother standing at the bench, sipping a cup of tea.

'Morning.' He kissed her cheek.

'Hi. Where's Mike? He's usually up by now.'

'He slept over at Stasy's house.'

'Really?' Katherine was surprised. 'Did you want to call and make sure he's all right?'

'No. I trust Stasy. If there had been a problem, she'd have let me know.'

'You…trust Stasy.' Katherine shook her head and sighed. 'Well, well, well.'

'Meaning?'

'I never thought I'd see the day when you trusted another woman with your son.'

'Stasy's different. She has kids of her own. She knows how to deal with them. I've been observing her and she's as strict with her kids as I am with Mike.'

'Whose idea was it for him to stay over?'

'Actually, I think it was all three kids.'

'Well, well, well,' Katherine said again, and took another sip of her tea. Justin poured himself a cup from the teapot that was beneath one of his mother's knitted cosies and walked over to the small round table nearby. 'Have you looked in on your father this morning?'

'Yes. He's looking really well. The scar is healing nicely and everything appears to be on track for him making a full recovery.'

'He's been sleeping more soundly at night, too.'

'It's amazing the difference a week makes,' Justin murmured.

'Are you talking about your father or about Stasy Roberts?'

'Hmm…both, but more about Stasy, I guess.'

'You must really like her.'

'I do, Mum. When Rose died, I never thought I'd be able to move on. I never thought I'd be able to meet a woman who touched me, who stirred me deep inside, but…' He trailed off and pushed both hands through his hair before lacing them behind his head and stretching his legs.

'She's been through a lot, Justin. You're going to have to take it very slowly with her.'

'I realise that.'

'Good, but can you do it? I mean, with your track record.'

'What track record? The only woman I've rushed to the altar was Rose.'

Katherine smiled. 'And we were all expecting her to deliver a baby within seven months after the wedding, you were so quick.'

'Ah, never eventuated, did it? Mike was born a good two years after we married. I told you she wasn't pregnant.'

'I know that, son.' Katherine laughed and Justin realised it was good to see his mum smiling again. 'But with Stasy, she doesn't trust easily.'

'How well do you know her?'

'Well enough. We grew quite close after her parents died. Poor girl really felt she had the weight of the world on her shoulders then, with having to support Skye was well as herself and the children.'

'She's supporting Skye? Financially?'

'Yes.'

'I hadn't realised.' He paused. 'She's quite a woman.'

'Yes, she is and she deserves the best.'

'You don't think that's me?'

'Oh, I do, darling. I'm totally biased when it comes to you. Any woman would be lucky to have you, Justin.'

'But?'

'But are you sure? Are you really sure she's the one? I don't want *you* getting hurt either, not when you've already been through so much.'

'All I know,' he said, choosing his words thoughtfully, 'is that Stasy has come to mean a lot to me in a very short time. I wasn't looking for an attachment but the fact that I've found one isn't something I'm going to deny. She's helped me to see that you need to go on with life. It moulds you, it changes you and just seeing the way she's looked after her children, her career, her sister, her property *and* herself... the woman's amazing.

'She's a brilliant doctor and I have the highest respect for her professionally and as a woman... well, let's just say that the physical attraction is definitely there. She's a survivor and she's done it tough. I admire that about her. I want to have her around because seeing that inner strength she exudes has made me realise mine could be stronger. She would be able to continue to help me with that and I'd be able to help her to loosen up a little bit more. Mum, if I've been granted a second chance or, as Skye put it, if I've picked up an ace, then I'm going to go with that royal flush.'

Katherine's smile was bright, her wise eyes

filled with tears of happiness as she nodded at her son. *'Carpe diem*, my darling.'

Justin stood and drained his cup, his words determined. 'I intend to, Mum.'

Justin turned up at Stasy's house just after eight-thirty and within ten minutes they were sitting down at her large wooden table, eating pancakes. The noise, the chatter, the excitement of the children filled Justin with a sense of happiness. As he looked around the table, he began to see the beginnings of a family but he quickly filed those thoughts away. He needed to take things slowly.

'So you two had a good time last night?' Skye asked after the kids had run off to play outside before the forecast rain came to spoil their fun.

'I certainly did,' Justin said as he carried his plate to the dishwasher and began stacking it.

'Oh, leave that,' Stasy immediately said, but Justin continued.

'You cooked, I'll clean up.'

'I like him more and more,' Skye said, not bothering to lower her voice. Stasy shot her a look but she ignored it. 'So come on, Stase. You haven't told me anything about last night. The kids have told me all about the cave and how they enjoyed dinner and the video games, but you've hardly said a word.'

'I had a good time,' she admitted, glancing at Justin. He met her gaze and winked at her, making her feel all girly and tingling inside. How could he do that with just one look?

'Although it was cut short when Alison went into labour,' Justin added.

'Really? Boy or girl?'

'Girl.' Stasy gave her sister the details while watching Justin. He looked comfortable in her kitchen, wiping down the benches and ensuring everything was in its place. When he'd finished, he came and sat at the table, bringing Stasy a fresh cup of coffee. 'Milk, no sugar. Right?'

'You remembered?'

'Does that impress you?'

'It does.'

'Impresses me, too,' Skye said. 'But that's irrelevant so I'll go study. I have finals in less that twelve weeks and six assignments to do.'

After Skye had left, Justin took Stasy's hand in his and lifted it to his lips, kissing her knuckles tenderly. Her breathing instantly became shallow and her smile was a shy one. 'Did you dream about me?' His voice was soft, intimate and it didn't help her to get control over her senses one little bit.

'Yes.'

'I dreamt about you, too.' He rubbed his thumb over the back of her hand with such tender affection she couldn't help being totally mesmerised by him.

'Should we be saying such things?' she whispered.

'I think we should.'

'Why? It only serves to confuse me even more, Justin.'

'No, Stasy. It serves to help you realise you're a very attractive, very sexy woman who has way too much loneliness in her eyes.' He tugged her out of her chair, standing up himself and drawing her close, into his arms. He didn't say anything but simply enfolded her warmly against him, closing his eyes. He couldn't help but feel her soft pliant body against his but this embrace wasn't about that. Justin wanted to show her there was more between them than just a physical reaction.

It was there, no doubt about that. The physical attraction between them was ever increasing but as she placed her arms about his waist, then slid them up the firm contours of his back, Stasy was astounded at how incredible it felt simply to be held like this…close to someone…someone she cared about.

As they stood there, she allowed herself to rest her head on his chest, listening to his heart beating steadily. This man had been through so much and yet he seemed willing to take a step forward, to appreciate what was in the past but at the same time look to the future. She admired that and envied it at the same time.

Neither of them spoke. This wasn't about words, it was about security. It was about letting her know she need not be alone any more. He'd known for years, had included it in one of his textbooks, the importance of touch to a human being. A reassuring hand on a shoulder, ruffling a child's hair, a supporting arm to lean on. Doctors applied the healing *touch* to their patients and nine times out of ten it had nothing to do with medicine. Being interested in someone, listening to them talk, to their stories, was as much a part of the recovery process as was the actual medication they prescribed.

He continued to hold her, feeling her slowly relax against him, feeling her touch on his back become one of thanks. They stood there for at least five minutes, the sound of the clock ticking, the faint noise of the children playing outside, the two of them absorbed into their own little world.

Stasy was the first one to make a move and when she pulled back she sniffed and looked up at Justin. A lone tear had escaped from each eye which he tenderly brushed away with the back of his hand.

'Thank you.' She sniffed again. 'It's been a long time since anyone's held me like that.'

'I figured.'

'How? How do you seem to know me so well?'

'The same way you seem to know me so well, Stasy.'

'But I've done nothing.'

'Not true. You've accepted me.'

'That's not difficult to do, Justin.'

'Not for *you*.' He stroked her head, enjoying not only the feel of her silky tendrils but the fact that she was letting him touch her in such an intimate way. 'You accept people as they are and that's a very rare quality to find. People are always wanting others to change. Their manners, their pigheadedness, their temper, their impatience, their clothes. The list goes on and on but not you. You meet someone and you simply accept them for who they are. That's a rare and precious quality, Stasy, and it's something I appreciate.

'I wasn't accepted as a person at my hospital in Melbourne. I was the *professor*. I was raised above others when it was the last thing I wanted. Staff were scared of me simply because of my title.'

'Scared of *you*?'

'See? You find that funny.'

'I find that a little astounding, yes.'

'That's because you see the good in everyone. Staff at Limestone Coast are still a little in awe of me but not you. Even though you had no idea who I was at the beginning, you still treated me normally. It's been a very long time since anyone has done that.'

'I still can't believe I didn't know.' She closed her eyes and shook her head, easing back slightly, but Justin wasn't ready to let her go completely. Not just yet.

'It wouldn't have made any difference.'

'You feel you know me that well?'

'You invited half the town to your children's birthday party!'

'Not half. You're exaggerating.'

'Actually, you probably invited the entire town but half of them were busy. You give to your children, your sister, the hospital…' Justin caressed her cheek then lifted her chin a little so their eyes could meet. 'Who gives to you, Anastasia?'

'I…er…' She tried to look away, feeling highly self-conscious and exposed.

'Don't. Don't pull away from me like that. I know my words probably make you feel uncomfortable but they shouldn't. You should be cared for. You *deserve* to be cared for. You should be able to *take* from someone, rather than being sucked dry with giving to everyone.'

Justin slid one hand around to the back of her neck, the other drew her back towards him. 'Take from me. Take comfort, take security, take protection.' *Take love*. Those were the next words he was about to say and they even had the power to stun him.

Love?

He was interested in Stasy, he liked her, he thoroughly enjoyed being with her, and he'd thought that perhaps in the next few weeks, as they continued to get to know each other, he would probably realise he was in love with her, but here? Now? So soon?

Yet there was no denying it and as his eyes dipped to take in the sight of her parted lips, the way her tongue slid out to wet them, inviting him to partake of their sweetness, he found he could no longer resist.

'I *need* to kiss you.'

Even hearing him say that made her insides liquefy and her breathing increase. She parted her lips, allowing the pent-up air to escape. She reached out and put a hand on his chest but she made no effort to push him away. Instead, it was as though she was drawing him close, wanting him closer, needing him closer.

As his head lowered, drawing ever nearer to hers, she closed her eyes and waited, trying to ignore the voice of reason, the pounding of indecision and fear that were clouding her mind, along with the desire and passion Justin was evoking.

'I know I'm rushing us both but I can't go any longer wondering what it might be like. My dreams of you will be nothing in comparison to the real thing but right now...I want to know.'

It was becoming increasingly difficult to breathe and her whole body was attuned to what was passing between them, connecting on a level neither had experienced before. 'I can't deny how incredible you make me feel.'

'I know.' He was so close now she could feel his breath on her face but she remained where she was, eyes closed again, face turned upwards to meet his. Her arms were once more around his waist, her hands touching the firm contours of his back, and this time she allowed her fingertips to caress, to learn, to enjoy.

'You're beautiful, Stasy.'

Before she could respond, before she could say or even think anything else, Justin pressed his lips softly against hers, brushing ever so lightly and tantalising her further. He didn't draw back but instead kept his mouth on hers, not moving, not pressuring but simply experiencing the way she felt, the way she tasted and trembled. It was intoxicating.

A slight tremor passed through her and it was enough to break the control he was working hard to exhibit. With that, he felt a little more need, a little more urgency driving him on, and he deepened the kiss.

For the first time in her life Stasy floated. Never had anyone kissed her with such abandonment and she not only accepted it, she reciprocated it, wanting to let Justin know that this moment was as important to her as it obviously was to him. She wanted it to go on being perfect as he continued to sweep her up into uncharted emotions as their mouths became more familiar with each other.

When he eventually drew back, both were panting. He rested his forehead against hers as they slowly came back to earth. 'Who would have thought?'

'Thought what?'

'That your mouth would be the perfect fit for mine.' Justin opened his eyes and edged back slightly to look at her.

'Mmm.' She murmured. 'Perfect.' She knew she should figure out what came next but her mind was too cloudy to either care or understand at the moment. All she knew was that Justin filled her senses, wholly and completely.

For the next two weeks she saw a lot of Justin both at work and after hours. He and Mike came for dinner at least twice a week and on Saturday nights Justin took them all out for dinner. The geology project the children were working hard on was really coming together and this was another reason why Mike was spending more and more time at her place.

'Mike's totally relaxed and at ease now,' Katherine said one afternoon when Stasy had dropped in to see Herb for herself. She had been pleased to see Justin's father was talking again, being careful with his bruised larynx and promising everyone to always chew his food properly from now on, and now they were all chatting in the cosy sitting room.

'After Rose's death, the poor lad withdrew completely into a little shell of his own,' Katherine continued. 'Justin was beside himself with concern and tried everything he could to help Mike.'

'He was…what? Six back then?'

'Yes, or almost six. I'd have to work it out.'

'Still, it's a very young age.'

'You were younger,' Katherine pointed out.

'I was too young to even remember. Mike

has clear memories of his mother and that's so precious.'

'At first Justin wasn't sure whether to talk about Rose or avoid the topic completely, but for himself he needed to talk, needed to remember. Mike, however, would clam up the instant anyone mentioned his mother. It was a very difficult time for everyone.'

'I'm sure.'

'Coming here, though, was the best thing they could have done, not only for Mike but for Justin as well.'

'You mean in decreasing his workload?'

'No, dear. I mean in meeting you. He's smitten is my son.'

'Smitten?' Stasy sat up straighter at the word. Was he really and what exactly did that mean? During the past few weeks since they'd began dating, Stasy knew her emotions were entwining themselves firmly around Justin but she wasn't in love. She couldn't be because she wouldn't let herself be. She'd been hurt so badly before and whilst Justin was the polar opposite of Wilt, she found it difficult to even think of surrendering to someone again.

'Yes, dear, but that's just a mother's perception and what mother doesn't want to see her son happy again? You've brought him back to life. Oh, he was happy enough when he arrived here but there was still a part of him he'd locked away and you've managed to not only find the key but to fit it into the lock and set him free.'

'Oh.' Stasy searched for something to say and failed.

Katherine and Herb both laughed. 'You're a special person, Stasy. Justin needs you, dear, and personally I think you need him, too.'

'Don't pressure the girl, Kath,' Herb said softly.

Katherine leaned forward and patted Stasy's hand. 'I can see I've scared you and perhaps I shouldn't have said as much as I have but, remember, you just take your time. Don't let him or us or the kids or Skye or anyone rush you. You'll figure things out in good time. Don't fret.'

Stasy was touched by their concern and nodded, unable to speak for a second due to the lump in her throat. The front door opened and Justin walked in, happy to find her there.

'I thought that was your car out front.' He beamed, quickly removing his wet coat and hanging it up. He crossed to Stasy's side and pressed a quick kiss to her cheek. She felt self-conscious at the public act in front of his parents but neither of them seemed to mind and Justin certainly didn't, so she told herself not to worry about it either. Easier said than done.

'You're home earlier than expected,' Katherine remarked, and Justin raised the brief-case he was holding and patted it.

'Thought I'd get more work done here than at the hospital with its constant interruptions, although now that I've found my girlfriend here, I doubt I'll get anything done.'

Girlfriend? Stasy stared at him as though he'd grown another head. He'd never called her that before but she guessed she *was* indeed his girlfriend. It just seemed like a word teenagers used, not people their age.

Justin came and sat down next to her, placing his arm along the back of the lounge as his mother asked him about his day. Stasy had been at the hospital that morning, doing the pre-dawn shift, and was starting to get a little tired…as well as being unable to shake those self-conscious feelings.

After a few minutes she stood. 'I'd better get going,' she said, stepping away from the lounge.

'Already?'

'I've been here for a while, Justin,' she said. 'Besides, it's time for your dad's medication and for him to have a rest.'

'She's right,' Herb said softly, and Stasy silently thanked him.

'OK.' Justin stood. 'I'll walk you out.'

'Thank you for visiting, Stasy,' Katherine said, coming over to give her a quick hug. 'Come any time.'

'Thanks, Katherine.'

Stasy pulled on her coat and scarf before taking her keys from her bag, getting ready to head out into the winter wet. After they stepped outside onto the front porch, Justin quickly picked up the umbrella he'd left by the door.

'Here.' He flicked it up then slipped his arm about her waist, drawing her close as they headed out to her car. She loved the feel of him so close, loved the way his scent surrounded her, loved the way he treated her with such honesty and respect.

'Everything all right when you left the hospital?' she asked.

'Gene has everything under control. He's going to do fine on his final exams, too.'

'Been helping him study?'

'Kind of. More like pointing him in the right direction as to what to swot up on.'

'Let me guess. You helped write the exam paper.'

'Many years ago.'

She shook her head slightly as they walked around to the driver's door. 'I keep forgetting you're a genius.'

'Hardly, Stasy.'

'My professor,' she said, and smiled up at him.

'You haven't called me that in a while.'

'I guess that's because I don't see you in that way any more.'

'Good, because I don't see you as just another colleague.' He bent his head and brushed his lips over hers in the most tantilising and feather-light touch, which made Stasy's head spin. She leaned into him and he instantly supported her. 'It's cold and wet. Drive carefully.'

'I will.'

'Call me later?'

'Yes.' Their evening chats had become a necessity to her and her loneliness had all but vanished. He was such a wonderful man, she thought as she waved and drove off. They were taking things slowly, really getting to know each other, giving the children time to adjust to seeing them together, but still Stasy felt things weren't right. She loved being with him, spending time with him, talking to him about anything and everything…so why did she feel the need to withdraw? Why couldn't she simply acknowledge and embrace what was happening between them?

'Because you're in love with him,' she whispered, shocking herself with the revelation.

CHAPTER NINE

THE following weekend, Justin was scheduled to work both days but was free in the evenings. The children had finished their school project and received an excellent mark and Mike had taken to sleeping over every Friday night. He'd brought over some of his clothes and Tim had cleared out a drawer for his friend, happy to have a 'brother-from-another-mother', as he termed it, at last!

Stasy had wondered whether Chelsea's nose might have been pushed a little out of joint at this new male bonding but she didn't seem at all bothered by it, treating Mike the same way she treated Tim. It was strange and almost as though Mike was the missing part of the puzzle. Was Justin the missing part in her puzzle?

Stasy pushed the thought away as she browned meat on the stove and added spices, before setting the pot to simmer. She looked at the clock, expecting Justin to arrive at any moment, and started to get a little fluttering in the pit of her stomach at the thought of seeing him soon. She still hadn't come to terms with the fact that she was in love with him mainly because she was unsure what was going to happen if he ever found out. He would, of course. She knew that. The more time they spent together, the stronger her feelings became, yet she still felt in a state of flux.

When she was with him, especially if it was just the two of them and the children, she felt fine, comfortable. If someone else was around, she was highly conscious of the way Justin would touch her, or put his arm about her shoulders or draw her close for a cuddle or hold her hand. At the hospital, of course, they were both professional and she appreciated that. Wilt had never been one to show affection in public and while she'd known her parents had loved her, they hadn't been overly demonstrative either.

She checked the clock again and heard the sound of his car outside, sloshing up her muddy driveway, which seemed to resemble a swamp more than a dirt track. Thankfully, tonight, Skye was having the evening off from studying and had gone out to dinner with her university friends. Stasy would be able to have Justin all to herself and she was looking forward to that. The kids didn't count. They were all so much a part of herself and Justin that it didn't bother them at all to go on dates or have a night in with three children in tow. It was just part of their lives.

'Hi,' he said, coming in the back door in his socks, having left his shoes outside on the verandah. He walked into the kitchen and gathered Stasy into his arms, pressing a smacking kiss to her lips. 'I missed you today.'

'You're the one who does the rosters, boss.'

'I know.' And the main reason why he'd rostered himself on this weekend was because he sensed Stasy was feeling a little closed in. He'd hoped that some time away from him might help her sort things out in that over-thinking mind of hers. 'How was your day?'

'So-so. I've filled the biscuit tins and made a tea-cake for dessert.'

'Excellent.' He patted his stomach. 'Mum says I'm putting on weight.'

Stasy slid her arms around his waist, instantly feeling the heat of his body affect her, causing her breathing to increase. She was still astounded that she had permission to touch him in such a familiar way and as she looked up into the rich, brown depths of his eyes, seeing them ignite with repressed desire, she was excited by the power she held over him. 'I don't feel any difference,' she said, not surprised that her voice sounded deeper and huskier than usual. 'Besides, I like the way you feel and that's all that counts, right?'

'Lady, you read my mind,' he murmured and dipped his head for another kiss.

'Oh, yuck. You're at it *again*?' Chelsea asked as she rounded the corner into the kitchen. Of course, that didn't stop her from coming over and squeezing between the two of them, putting her arms about them both. They hugged the girl back, Chelsea resting her head on Justin for a moment before looking up at her mother.

'Do I have to have a shower?'

'Yes.'

'But I had one this morning.'

'Yes, and that was before you drew on your leg.'

'She drew on her leg?' Justin asked.

'Mum. No.' Chelsea shook her head, a little embarrassed.

'Show Justin what you did.' Stasy couldn't help the chuckle that bubbled up.

'Do I have to?'

'Yes. It's funny but it's also the reason why you need to have another shower.'

Reluctantly, Chelsea lifted up the hem on the

play-skirt she wore so it was just above her knee. There at the top of her knee was a large navy blue circle, completely coloured in.

'What did you do that for?' Justin asked, totally perplexed.

'I had a big hole in the tights I was wearing this morning and I didn't want anyone to see so I—'

'Coloured it in,' he finished for her, his lips tugging into a smile. Stasy dropped a hand around Chelsea's shoulders.

'Is my girl a thinker or is my girl a *thinker*?'

'Mum! It's not funny.'

'No.' She dropped a kiss on Chelsea's blonde head. 'It's ingenious. Only problem is once you remove the tights, it does look a bit odd to be walking around with a blue circle on your leg.' She patted the nine-year-old's bottom. 'Shower. Do you need me to run it for you?'

'Yes.'

'I'll monitor dinner,' Justin said.

As Stasy headed off, she looked back to see him stirring the pasta sauce she'd made, sniffing and sticking his little finger in to taste it. 'Mmm,' he murmured and that one little action, the fact that he loved her cooking, made him even more special to her.

He liked her cooking. He liked her eyes. He liked the way she laughed. He liked to dream about her. The man was everything *she'd* always dreamed of, so why did she still have this wall in front of her that she didn't seem able to get past? There was no need to hide the fact that they were dating from the children because the children had figured it all out on their own and were more than happy to see their respective parents together.

After Chelsea had finished in the shower, they had dinner together and then noticing the three children were rather restless, Justin suggested they go out.

'Where?' Stasy asked amid the cheering of the children. 'It's raining.'

'No. It's stopped. First time in days,' he said, pointing out the window. They all peered out into the evening light. The moon was full and, much to her surprise, she found Justin was right.

'It's still cold,' she pointed out.

'We can rug up. Call it a treat for the kids doing so well in their school project.'

'OK, then. Kids, get your coats and scarves and gloves and beanies.' She turned to look at Justin. 'Where do you want to go?'

He shrugged. 'What is there to do on a Saturday night in Mount Gambier for two adults and three children?'

'Hmm. There's Umpherston's?' Stasy ventured.

'Of course. Yes! I'd forgotten all about that place.' His smile was reminiscent and he chuckled to himself. 'It's been for ever since I've been there. Is it still a cool place for teenagers to hang out?'

'Perhaps in summer.' Stasy smiled at him and shook her head.

'What?' he asked, noting her expression.

'You're still a big kid at heart.'

'So?' He pulled her into his arms. 'Isn't that what you love about me?'

At his words, she stilled. How could he know that? Was it written all over her face? Panic began to rise within her. If Justin thought she loved him then he'd want her to take their relationship to the next step and she wasn't sure she was ready for that.

'Does Umpherston's still have possums?'

Stasy shifted slightly and sneaked a glance at his face. Had what he'd said been just a throwaway line? He didn't seem confused or concerned about anything. She started to relax, realising he wasn't about to drop to one knee and propose. If he did, she had no idea how she'd react.

'Stasy?' he asked when she didn't reply.

'Huh? Possums? Er…yes.' She eased out of his hold and went into the kitchen.

'What are you doing?'

'Making some possum food.'

'Possum food?'

'Bread and honey. It's their favourite. Apples are put out every night so they don't starve in case the people who go to visit don't bring food with them but it's the bread and honey those little furry fellas crave.' She busied herself in the kitchen.

Justin watched as she seemed to flit around and wondered what he could do to help calm her nerves. He'd felt the way she was starting to distance herself from him, not all the time, just every now and then. She'd stiffened in his arms just now when he'd mentioned the word 'love'. Didn't she *want* to be loved? Didn't she *want* to love him back?

He pondered the thoughts as they all bundled into the car and drove to the large vertical sink hole. They descended the ivy-covered steps to the floor below, Stasy handing out the possum food for the kids to distribute.

'This is marvellous. Better than I remembered,' he said as they walked around the well-lit area of the beautifully tiered garden. 'Were the possums always that big?' Justin asked, after being startled by one.

'More than likely.' Stasy laughed at him, holding his hand. He was a little surprised at her initiating the contact but as they appeared to have the sink hole to themselves, she probably felt quite safe. He'd noticed she didn't like it all that much when he touched or kissed her in public, even in front of their family, but neither was he going to stop. He was a demonstrative man and he wanted the whole world to see how special he thought this woman next to him was.

They continued to walk around on the slightly uneven path, Stasy pointing out recent developments, like the little fountain that was bubbling away, while their children's voices echoed around the sink hole, all of them having fun.

Stasy saw a possum perched on a ledge in the jagged-swiss-cheese rock and held out a piece of bread. Two little paws with sharp claws reached out and took it from her. It didn't run away and hide to eat its prize but instead sat there and ate it in front of them, munching away happily.

'Were they always this tame?' Justin asked rhetorically.

Stasy led him over to a carved seat made from a long tree-log, not far from the fountain. They sat down and looked out at the gardens. The level below them was lined with lilies, agapanthus and other glorious plants and flowers, tucked up in their leaves to protect them from the cold. The level at the top was surrounded by hanging vines, most hugging the circumference of the sink hole.

'Where are the children?' Justin asked after a moment.

Stasy pointed them out as they ran around on the lower level, the floodlights depicting them clearly. 'They're having fun and thankfully…' she glanced around them '…it appears we have the place to ourselves, at least for the moment at any rate.'

Justin shifted on the hard wooden seat, wishing it wasn't so close to the ground and that the back had a higher and deeper cut. But here, in this place which some would say radiated majestic beauty, he didn't need to wish. He watched her looking out over the wide open space, watching the kids as they yelled and whooped with delight. She was smiling, enjoying the happiness reflected in her children. She was a beautiful woman and although he'd known that upon first meeting her, he now *felt* it because he'd been allowed to see into her soul. She was beautiful inside and out and he knew how rare a find that was. It seemed like so long ago since they'd met rather than just a few weeks. He breathed in deeply, filling his lungs all the way with the scent of Stasy.

He sat there, admiring her beauty rather than the garden's. A small gust of wind blew a few strands of hair across her cheek and he instantly reached out to brush it back, their hands colliding as she went to do the same thing.

'Sorry.' His tone was deep, intimate and it was that more than anything which made her turn to face him, her fingers still entangled with his. He brought his other hand up to push her hair behind her ear, keeping it out of the way. Gently, he caressed and smoothed it.

'Justin?'

He felt that apprehension again. 'Stasy, talk to me. Don't shut me out. Please?'

She sighed and looked away. 'I don't…I don't mean to shut you out. I guess it's more of a reflex than anything else.'

'You've been protecting yourself for so long? Is that why you shut me out?'

'Yes. Something like that.' She paused but Justin waited, stayed silent, and it was as though he was willing her to speak, willing her to open up. She'd known this conversation was coming, that it was inevitable, but she'd also hoped to push it aside for as long as possible. She knew that when she said what she had to say Justin would probably withdraw, would probably stop dating her and stop pursuing her all together. After all, what man wanted a woman who was broken on the inside?

She clutched her hands together and prayed for strength before turning to face him. 'I don't know if I can do this.'

'This? You and me?'

'Yes.'

'Why?' His voice was calm and interested, as though he were dealing with a medical problem he already knew how to fix.

'Justin, I've already been through one failed marriage and the heartache caused from it will be enough to last me for ever. I failed. Don't you understand that? I *failed* as a wife. I don't know how you feel about me and part of me doesn't want to know because if I do then…' She broke off, her voice choking on a sob. She shrugged. 'I don't know what to do. I don't want to hurt you, especially when you're so amazingly incredible and, you know…perfect.'

'You can't hurt me.'

'You say I've inspired you,' she went on, not really hearing his words. 'You say that you admire my strength and my survival instincts, but you're wrong. I'm not that woman.'

'Yes, you are.'

'I'm not. I fall apart at the seams—even now—when I think of how I failed.'

'That's natural.'

'No, it's not.'

'Yes, it is. Stasy, the breakdown of a marriage is one of the most stressful events that can happen to a person.'

'But it was eight years ago, Justin. Why aren't I over it yet?'

'You are.'

'How can you say that?'

'You're over the *divorce*, Stasy. It's quite clear that you're not still in love with your ex-husband. Are you?'

'Definitely not.'

'There you go. You've moved on with your life and by that I don't mean dating or me or what's happening between us. I mean you're not mentally or emotionally at the same place you were eight years ago.'

'No.'

'You've faced a lot of ups and downs, especially in the last few years since your parents died and Skye came to live with you.'

'Yes, but if I'm over all of this, if I've moved on, as you say, why do I seem to have this block when it comes to you?'

'Oh, Stasy.' He drew her closer, slipping his arm about her shoulders. 'You don't have a block, honey. You're just having trouble stepping into the light. I know what it's like.'

'Really? You've been through this?'

'Yes.'

'Well what helped you to take that last step?'

'You did.'

'Me?' Stasy shook her head. 'That makes no sense.'

'It makes a lot of sense. Stasy, my wife didn't leave me. She died. My marriage was a happy one and although it came to an end, I wasn't bitter afterwards. I was grief stricken, I was lost for a while but Mike brought me back to earth with a quick thud. Having to take care of him, having to be there for him really helped me, just as I'm sure your kids helped you.'

'They did. I didn't have time to think back then, they were both so little. Add to that fact I was trying to maintain a medical career and...' She trailed off and sighed. 'It was hard.'

'And, no doubt, you've pushed a lot of the emotions you otherwise would have dealt with before now to the back of your mind. You focused on the day-to-day running of your life and that routine, that control is what has got you through. Until now. You may have moved on with your life but now that you're contemplating taking a step into the unknown, all those old doubts and insecurities have raised their ugly heads again.'

What he said made sense and she closed her eyes, leaning more firmly against him, wanting to absorb his words. 'Tell me more, Professor.'

She felt him smile at that. It was odd. She knew him so well that she could tell when he was smiling even though he hadn't said anything, even though she couldn't see his face.

He didn't say anything for a few seconds but when he did, it wasn't what she'd expected. 'When Rose died, I thought my heart would never heal. Of course it did. Time really does heal all wounds, but the time is different for everyone. I never thought I'd meet another woman I wanted to be with yet within a short time of moving here, I met you. I can see that inner strength you possess and I know you'll be fine. I know whatever it is you're facing, whatever obstacles are in your way, you'll leap over them with plenty of room to spare.

'You've told me you've been lonely, which is quite understandable, but you've also taken steps to counteract that loneliness. You give to everyone around you and that does help. Again, I know because I've been there but I also know you can feel the most alone when in a crowd.

Lonely people can make such awe-inspiring attempts to lift their loneliness by becoming too involved but at the same time not letting anyone become involved with *them*.'

'What if they're just plain scared?'

'Scare of getting hurt again?'

'That…and of doing the hurting.' She pulled back and looked up at him then, her eyes filled with earnestness. 'I don't want to hurt you.'

'You *won't*.'

'But what if I do?'

'You won't.'

'How do you know that?'

'Because I've picked up another ace.'

Stasy stilled at his words and he could sense her starting to withdraw again. 'No. Don't.' His tone was slightly pleading. 'Don't pull away from me. Open up. Tell me what you're thinking.'

'You're…scaring me, Justin.'

'Why is that?'

Stasy swallowed, wanting to say the words but not knowing how. What if she was wrong?

What if she'd completely picked up the wrong signals, the wrong end of the stick? But she couldn't have. His mother had told her he was smitten with her. He'd just told her he'd picked up another ace. That could only mean one thing and she wasn't sure she was ready to hear it.

'Why?' he persisted. 'Why am I scaring you?'

'Because you're about to tell me that you…that you…' She stopped, her breathing too rapid.

'That I love you?'

'Yes.' The word was a whisper.

'I do.'

'You do?'

'I do,' he repeated. 'Took me quite by surprise but there it is and now that I've actually come out and said those three little powerful words, has it changed anything?'

'Yes.'

'How?' Again his tone was calm and controlled.

'Now I don't know what you expect of me. Do you expect me to say those words back to you?'

'Can you?'

'I…I don't know.'

He nodded and she thought she saw a glimmer of hesitation in his resolve, but it was gone so quickly she wondered if she'd imagined it. 'The thing is, I didn't tell you I love you to make you feel trapped.'

'Then why? Why did you have to say it?'

'So you'd know how I felt, that this attraction between us isn't just some short-term fling. I love you and I want you to know it. Life is far too uncertain, Stasy. That lesson I learned the hard way. Too many people take life for granted. You and I, we see death on a regular basis but when you experience such gut-wrenching loss…it changes you.

'Meeting you, I've been given a second chance. Your father found love twice and, just like him, I've picked up another ace and I'm not letting it go. So I'll be patient. I'll not rush you and I'll be here when you're ready.'

'Ready to do what? I still don't know.'

'And when you do, I'll be here.'

She was sure his words were probably meant to reassure her but instead they served to scare her even more. What if she didn't ever sort herself out? What if all she had room for in her life were her children, her sister, her work? It was true that Justin and Mike seemed to have slotted into their lives with ease but that didn't mean a full-time relationship, a *marriage* would work out between them.

Stasy closed her eyes again, her head starting to pound with the pressure.

Could she do it? Could she take the leap off that cliff into the unknown?

CHAPTER TEN

WHEN her cellphone rang it scared her, making her jump, and because Justin was so close, they knocked heads. With both of them groaning, rubbing their foreheads and laughing, the previous mood broke. Stasy answered her call. 'Dr Roberts.'

'Stasy.' Gene's voice was urgent on the other end of the line. 'There's been a boat accident on the Glenelg River. A tourist boat caught fire. We've only just received word but I'm going to need you soon. We're going to have casualties lining the walls.'

'Right. Thanks for the heads up. Justin's here with me so we'll come in together once we've dropped the children off.'

'Emergency?' Justin asked when she'd rung off.

'Yes.'

'What do you want to do with the kids? Would Skye be home yet?' Justin asked as they called the children over.

'No, and it's not fair to ask her to come home. She rarely gets a night out.'

'Why don't they all go to my parents' house? That way Tim and Chelsea can have a sleep with Mike for once.'

Stasy hesitated. 'What about your dad?'

'He'll enjoy it, too,' Justin said with a smile as they started up the steps. 'I'll give them a call.' Justin took out his phone and called his parents. Katherine spoke loud enough for Stasy to hear that they'd love to have the children.

'She's getting it all organised,' Justin said as they climbed into the car.

'Getting what organised?' Chelsea asked. Stasy quickly explained the situation, not sure how her two would feel about going somewhere else, but the delight which met the proposed scheme settled things rather quickly.

As Justin started to drive, the rain started up again and when he pulled up at his parents' house, they all quickly rushed inside.

'Don't give Mike's grandparents a hard time,' Stasy warned, looking pointedly at both children. 'Go to bed when Katherine tells you to and remember your manners.'

'Yes, Mum,' they said in unison.

'Right. Now, give me a hug.'

'Will we be here all night?' Chelsea asked, the delight at the prospect reflected in her blue eyes.

'Probably.'

'How exciting!' She squeezed her mother's neck before running off to play in Mike's room.

'Go,' Katherine said, all but pushing her out of the door. 'They'll be fine.'

Stasy nodded and rushed to the car where Justin was waiting. The windscreen wipers were working overtime as they headed to the hospital.

'Looks like we're in for a wet night,' he murmured, and reached for her hand. He brought it to his lips and kissed it. 'That was very brave, leaving your children with someone else overnight. *Big* step outside your comfort zone.'

Stasy merely nodded, unable to talk about it at the moment as she was trying to get her head around it.

'I just wanted you to know I'm impressed.' He pulled up outside the hospital and cut the engine.

'You are?'

'Yes.' His smile was warm and encouraging and it filled Stasy with strength.

'Thanks, Justin.' She leaned over and brushed a quick kiss across his lips. 'Perhaps I'm not as strong as you think I am.'

'Impossible.' He smiled, winked at her then climbed from the car, bringing an umbrella around to the passenger side and walking with her into the hospital.

'We'll need to get into retrieval suits,' Stasy said, leading the way to where the bright orange suits were stored and handing him one. 'Let's go see how Gene handles his first official briefing.' Four paramedics, already dressed in retrieval gear, were waiting for them. 'Sorry to hold you up.' Stasy nodded for Gene to proceed.

'Thank you. The report came in twenty minutes ago now. We've received word that both police and fire crews are in attendance. Bateman's Cruises were taking fifteen people out for a night cruise on the Glenelg River when there was an explosion on the boat. At this stage, the actual cause of the explosion is unknown. Thankfully, the cruise was almost over and they were on their way back to shore. Several people are injured and actually managed to swim to shore. The police were taking a boat out to check on anyone still in the cruise boat. Stasy and Justin, you'll need to deal with the worst cases first—my guess would be the ones on the boat. As soon as I know more, I'll let you know.'

'What about Portland Hospital?' Stasy asked, pleased with the way her registrar was handling the situation.

'I've contacted them to say they'll be receiving casualties. Hopefully, between the two hospitals we should be able to handle the injuries and only the worst cases will need to be airlifted to Adelaide. I've called in extra nursing staff as well as notifying the surgeons who are presently in town that their services may be required.'

'Excellent.'

Stasy nodded. 'We'll get changed. Can you make sure the retrieval kits are out and ready?'

'Already done.' Gene pointed behind her where their kits stood, complete with spotlight hard hats and walkie-talkies.

'Great. Thanks, Gene.' As she headed to the changing rooms, Justin fell into step beside her.

'He did well.'

'Yes, he did. I'm prodigiously proud of him.'

'You've trained him well.'

'Thank you.' She grinned as she entered the female changing rooms, still surprised that she didn't feel self-conscious around Justin when she still expected to. She guessed that here at work they each knew their place and so there was no confusion, nothing out of the ordinary. She finger-combed her hair, pulling it back into a ponytail, knowing Justin would more than likely pull it out once they'd finished. It wouldn't be the first time he'd removed the band from her hair after she'd left the hospital.

'I like your hair out,' he'd said, running his fingers through it, and his words and actions had had the ability to make her forget everything else except the powerful emotions that existed between them.

As Justin drove them out to the accident site, they discussed what type of injuries they might find. It was easier to take one of their cars and follow the ambulance, especially as they weren't at all sure what they were going to find. Focusing on work was the best way she could think of to control her thoughts.

'Turn right here,' she instructed as they entered the road which would wind down the cliff towards the base where the river ran. 'Lots of floodlights already set up,' she murmured. 'Good. We can get the paramedics to deal with the little things such as abrasions and minor burns.'

'Hypothermia—especially if people have been swimming in that river.'

'Yes,' she agreed. 'I can do a quick triage if you like.'

'No. Appoint one of the paramedics to do the triage. If a boat has blown up, there's bound to be at least one or two people who will be in a bad way and they would have been the closest to the blast. I just wish the rain would let up.'

'I doubt it will.' Stasy looked around them as he brought the vehicle to a halt. 'I hope one of the badly hurt patients isn't a child.' She said the words softly but Justin reached out and put a hand on her shoulder, looking deeply into her face, which was partly illuminated by the searchlights set up outside.

'If it is, we'll deal with it. You and me. Together we make an amazing team, Dr Roberts.'

'Agreed, Professor Gray.'

He squeezed her shoulder in encouragement but before he could remove it she placed her hand over his and held it in hers. Neither of them moved and for a brief moment time stood still as they looked at each other. Trust, confidence and knowledge that they would not only cope but would work together like a well-oiled machine were definitely reflected in his eyes and once more she derived strength from him.

They burst into action, Justin heading over to speak to the police officer in charge, who was under a rigged-up shelter, while Stasy organised the paramedics.

'We have twenty people to deal with in total. Thirteen have managed to make it to the bank so that leaves seven out there still on the boat.

The police team have tried to bring the boat in but one man is in a bad way and every time the boat moves his pain levels soar so they're going to leave everything where it is until we can give him something for the pain. We'll try and keep the patients dry and get them moved out of here as soon as possible.' When Justin returned to her side, they swapped information.

'Right. And the boat's safe now? No more explosions?' she asked.

'The fire crews have put the fire out and surveyed the area, declaring it safe.'

'Good. Did they say who the patient is?'

'Daryl Bateman.'

Stasy gasped then swallowed slowly, thinking of the friendly guy who loved his job working on the boat. 'I guess this is the drawback to working in a small town,' she said softly. 'You'll eventually end up treating your friends.'

'You'll be as wonderful and as brilliant as usual, I have no doubt about that,' he encouraged her, and she smiled her thanks as they gathered their retrieval kits and headed out to their main patient.

Daryl was indeed in a bad way. Not only did he have extensive burns to his left and right hands as well as to the lower left side of his body, his hair was singed, his eyebrows were missing and he had a large piece of wood impaled in his right shoulder. A tarpaulin had been set up to keep as much rain off Daryl as possible.

'His clavicle looks fractured. Pupils equal and reacting to light.' Justin held out his hand. 'Stasy, pass me my stethoscope.'

She did as he asked before looking at Ernie Harris, Daryl's colleague, who was unconscious at the other end of the boat. The police had managed to retrieve the other five patients, which just left these two men as they were the worst and therefore needed the most attention.

'Ernie was being the hero,' Sergeant Vanessa Bell reported. 'There were two kids who wouldn't have been able to swim to shore, so he took each one to shore, then came back for their mother, ensuring the entire family was safe. As you can see, his left leg is injured but apparently, when he got back to the boat, intending to help someone else, he collapsed.'

Stasy felt Ernie's head. 'No big bumps. He obviously didn't hit it.' Her patient was covered with a space blanket over his wet clothes, his body extremely cool to the touch. 'I'd guess the water as well as exhaustion was what caused him to collapse.'

'It is freezing,' Vanessa confirmed. 'Then again, it is the end of August. The river is supposed to be freezing.'

Stasy was busy dealing with Ernie, checking his leg because the sooner she did that, the sooner they'd be able to shift him and get him warmer than they could do now. 'His temperature isn't too bad, thankfully not in the critical range,' she reported. 'Left tibia feels uneven, possibly fractured.'

'How did he do all that swimming, then?'

'Adrenaline. Plus the water would have numbed the pain.' As she spoke, Ernie coughed as he regained consciousness. 'Here he is.' When he tried to move, she placed a hand on him. 'Stay still. It's Stasy, Ernie,' she said clearly. 'Can you hear me?'

'Yeah, so stop yellin', Stasy. You're givin' me a headache.'

She smiled, pleased to see his sense of humour was still intact even though his voice was very faint. 'I'm going to give you something for the pain and then we'll get Vanessa to transfer you to the shore.'

'Righto, Doc. I'm glad you lot showed up. What a night, eh? I managed to get some of the little tackers to shore. Everyone off now?'

'Everyone's being attended to. You did good, Ernie. Real good, mate. Rest now.'

'Yeah. Yeah, I think I will.'

'Stasy? I need you,' Justin called, and she quickly administered Ernie's analgesic before shifting very carefully around the boat, stepping over bits of debris, towards where Justin was kneeling beside Daryl.

'Yes, Justin?'

'Do a check of Daryl's vitals, please. In this light, I'd prefer confirmation.' He held the torch for her, also shining the light from his hard hat in the same direction to give her the most light possible. She noted he'd done an excellent job of binding Daryl's shoulder, ensuring the large shard of wood that impaled the scapula was stable.

Stasy nodded and pulled out her own medical torch. 'Pupils still equal and reacting but sluggish,' she began, hooking the stethoscope in to her ears and listening. 'Lungs are fine. Airway is clear.' She carefully touched her hands to the back of Daryl's head, feeling for contusions. Her fingers were cold, wet and numb but she managed. 'Obvious burns, bruising and lacerations to his body. Impaled right shoulder.' She continued to feel the scalp. 'Depressed fracture.'

Daryl started to mumble again and she called to him but he was still unresponsive.

'Definite concussion,' she concluded then said with a bit more volume, 'Daryl? Can you open your eyes?'

Again he mumbled something but the response wasn't clear and his eyes remained closed. However, it was a response to her question.

'Check his ears,' Justin suggested, and she looked at him in the artificial light, trying to read his expression.

'This one of your famous hunches, Professor?'

'Yes.'

She checked on the side of Daryl's ear where the depressed fracture was located. 'Otorrhoea?' She reached into her kit which was closer than Justin's and ripped open a padded bandage, touching it to the side of Daryl's ear and neck. 'Yes. There's a definite drainage coming from the ear. It's tinged with blood.' She held it up to the light and they both took a quick look. 'Good call.' The man was an amazing medical machine. She knew she was good and would have picked up on Daryl's situation probably, given time and a bit more light, but Justin had a real gift for what he did and her love and appreciation for him soared. She respected him so much, she loved him so much and at that moment she had no idea how she could even have any second thoughts about a life with him.

'Look for bruising. I'm on the wrong side of him and it's difficult to manoeuvre around. I don't want to rock the boat—literally.'

She nodded and did as he asked. 'There it is. Battle's sign and it looks to be getting worse.'

'Basilar skull fracture. Right, we'll need to fashion a cervical collar before moving him. The manufactured ones are too bulky with his bandaged shoulder.'

'I'm on it,' she said, after they'd angled Daryl to his side as best they could so his ear could drain.

'There's no sign of fluid from the nose,' Justin

continued as he finished dealing with Daryl's burns, wrapping them to keep them isolated from the air and water. 'How much longer do you think it will be before we can move him?'

'About another five minutes.' She looked out to see the police rescue boat just reaching the shore with Ernie on board.

'Daryl will need to go to Adelaide. His injuries are too extensive, his Glasgow coma score is five. Not good. Limestone Coast Hospital doesn't have the proper equipment to deal with it and he'll require immediate specialised treatment,' he stated. 'Contact Gene and tell him to get that helicopter pilot off standby and arrange a meeting place close by.'

'On it,' she replied, and pulled out her cellphone, glad there was reception in this area. When that was done, she began packing up their equipment so they'd be ready once the boat returned. 'What do you think will be the best way to transfer Daryl?'

Justin thought for a moment before they

started discussing possibilities and options for keeping their patient as still and as stable as possible. For the most part, things went to the plan they'd devised and soon they were loading Daryl into the back of the ambulance.

They both went with the paramedics for the ten-minute drive to where the helicopter would meet them. As they left, two more ambulances from Portland turned up and Stasy felt more comfortable about leaving the accident site knowing there were a plethora of trained professionals to deal with the situation.

Stasy changed the drainage pad on Daryl's ear, still calling to him and getting varied responses.

'Better.' Justin unhooked the stethoscope from his ears, checked Daryl's pupils and made sure the airway was clear. 'So how old is he?'

'Um…thirty-eight. Same as me. I want to take a closer look at his bandage.' She held up the one she'd removed from Daryl's ear towards the artificial lights inside the ambulance, noting the halos around the drops of blood.

'Does it have a yellowish tinge?'

'Yes.'

'Cerebrospinal fluid present.'

'Yes.'

'Confirms basilar fracture and means that the fracture has crossed the temporal dura matter.' He shook his head slowly as he looked at their patient. 'We're going to get you help, Daryl. Don't you worry about that. We're going to take you to some of the best surgeons in Australia.'

'Vitals are still holding,' she said as she changed the bag of saline over. 'Otorrhoea has stabilised.'

'Good.'

'Are you happy to accompany Daryl to Adelaide?' she asked. 'I can head back to the hospital and manage things there until you return.'

Justin thought for a moment before nodding.

'That sounds like the best idea. It shouldn't take too long and then I can come back and help with the clean-up of smaller cases.'

'All right.' When they arrived at the nearby oval where the helicopter was just landing, Stasy and Justin transferred Daryl over. Yet when it came time for the helicopter to leave, Stasy couldn't believe how concerned she felt for Justin. It was still raining quite heavily. What if something happened to the helicopter? What if something happened to Justin?

As he turned to say goodbye to her, he found himself enveloped in a tight hug, his arms immediately going around Stasy's back and drawing her closer.

'You be careful.'

'I will.'

'You come back to me,' she ordered.

Justin smiled down into her wet face and brushed away from her cheek a few soaking hairs which had come loose. 'I will, honey. Don't you worry about that.'

Stasy's heart was pounding wildly against her chest and she found it almost impossible to let go of him. She had to tell him, she had to let him know how she felt. Could she? Could she do it? Take that final leap? She might get hurt, she might hurt him. There were three innocent children caught up in this as well but the urge to tell him what was in her heart was too great and, taking a deep breath, she gave in.

'I…I love you,' she finally said.

'Oh, Stasy.' Justin kissed her soundly. 'You're fantastic. Now, go and get back to the hospital, get into dry clothes and I'll see you soon.'

'What if you can't get back from Adelaide? What if the storm is too severe?'

'Justin?' the pilot called, and Justin nodded.

'Gotta go, my darling.' He kissed her again and let her go, climbing into the helicopter beside Daryl. Stasy walked away, ducking beneath the whirring rotors as she headed back to the ambulance. She watched the helicopter take off, taking away the man she loved, and if she'd thought she'd known loneliness before it was nothing compared to now.

CHAPTER ELEVEN

As it turned out, the helicopter had made it safely to Adelaide and from the reports Stasy had just received on Daryl's condition, he was currently in Theatre but was now out of critical danger.

'It doesn't look as though I'm going to be able to make it back until morning,' Justin said. 'It's bucketing down with rain here in Adelaide, too.'

Stasy was sitting in her office, having gone there to take his call.

'How's A and E? Quiet now?'

It was almost two o'clock in the morning and Stasy was glad the brunt of the emergency was now over. Patients had been seen and treated, specialists called in to deal with different situations and A and E was now relatively quiet. 'Yes.'

'Why don't you head home and try and get some sleep?' he suggested.

'I could get through some paperwork instead.'

'But you hate paperwork.'

'I just need to keep busy. Until you're back here with me, I need to keep busy.'

'Stasy, it's all right. I'll be back soon enough. Then we'll talk and we'll sort everything out.'

'Will we?'

'What's making you doubt?'

'Oh, Justin, I don't know. Anything. Everything. Nothing.'

'Confusing.'

'You're tell me. Try being in *my* head!'

'Do you doubt that I love you?'

'No.'

'Do you doubt that you love me?'

'No.'

Justin let out his breath and nodded. 'Then that's all that matters. Stasy, you're making progress. You're starting to let go of your past. Keep doing that. I'm right there by your side…' He paused then chuckled. 'Figuratively at the moment but there nonetheless.'

'I miss you.' Her words were soft and quiet and Justin's impatience at their present situation increased.

'I miss you, too.'

'When you left…when that helicopter took off in that storm…' Stasy closed her eyes, tears forming beneath her lashes. 'I've never felt so lonely. I need you, Justin. I really need you. You've changed my life, you've turned it from being upside down to right side up and I need you. I couldn't let myself need anyone in the past. I had to be strong. First of all for the children and then later for my sister.'

'Now you can lean on me and I'll lean on you.' He closed his eyes, hoping she could hear the truth of his feelings in his voice. 'Go home, Anastasia. Call me when you get there. I'll keep working on a way out of here.'

Her eyes snapped open. 'Don't rush it, though. Don't go taking unnecessary risks.'

'Not about to happen,' he said with a laugh. 'I finally have a good hand of cards and I'm not about to be careless with them. Call me soon,' he said, before hanging up.

Stasy pushed the paperwork aside, deciding she'd much rather think about Justin. He'd said she could lean on him and that he'd lean on her. That sounded suspiciously like the suggestion for an equal relationship and that was something she knew she hadn't had with Wilt.

'He's worth it,' she told herself as she picked up her bag. 'He's worth taking the chance.'

When she arrived home, she walked slowly around the house. She'd received a text message from Skye to say she was spending the night at a friend's so that meant no one was there. She switched on the lights of her children's bedrooms, looking at their mess and their empty beds. She couldn't ever remember a time when she'd been in this house by herself,

alone on a dark and stormy night. The oddest
thing was that she didn't feel lonely at all.
Many a time she'd sat in the darkened lounge
room at night and felt so desolate she'd had
pains in her chest. Now all she could see were
the signs of love all around her. The posters of
rock stars on Chelsea's bedroom walls, the car
and motorbike pictures on Tim's. Skye's desk
was filled with a mound of papers mixed with
textbooks. There was love in this house and
Stasy realised how much of that love belonged
to her.

She loved her children and her sister so dearly
and she knew she was loved in return. Now she
could add Justin and Mike to that list and she
knew they reciprocated her feelings. Katherine
and Herb were there, too, providing that
parental base both she and Skye had lost. In
loving Justin, she'd gained so much and tears
of happiness slid down her cheeks.

She went through the motions of getting
ready for bed then called Justin and talked to

him for an hour until her eyes began to close and her words started to slur.

'Sleep, my dearest Anastasia,' he murmured. 'I'll be home and in your arms soon enough.'

'I love you, Justin,' she whispered on a yawn.

'I love you, too.'

Stasy woke to the sound of a loud crack and sat bolt upright in bed. 'What was that?'

The rain was still coming down outside and she settled back amongst the pillows, realising it had probably been thunder that had woken her. She checked the clock and was astounded to find it was after nine. She looked down at her hand, surprised to find it still holding the phone and she smiled, remembering the relaxing conversation she'd had with Justin. They'd talked about nothing in particular and everything at the same time. It was wonderful.

She quickly called Katherine to check on the

children and was told they'd been up for hours, had had their breakfasts and were watching television. Stasy spoke to all three of them and could hear the happiness in their voices that reassured her they were indeed all right. 'Don't rush, dear,' Katherine said after Stasy had spoken to Mike. 'Take your time. Sleep in and pamper yourself a bit. The children are more than welcome to stay until lunchtime so I've suggested to Justin that once he's back he goes to pick you up first and that way you can have a bit of time to yourselves.'

'You've spoken to Justin?'

'He called about ten minutes ago to say the weather was starting to lift in Adelaide and he should be home soon.'

Why hadn't he called her?

'He thought you might have slept in and said he'd call you just before the helicopter took off.'

'Oh. OK, then.' He might be trying to call her now. 'Well, if the children are being no trouble, I guess I'll see you for lunch.'

'I'm looking forward to it, dear.'

Stasy quickly went and had a shower, taking the phone into the bathroom with her just in case Justin called. By the time she was dressed, he still hadn't called so she decided to call him instead.

'Hi,' he said. 'Was just about to ring.'

'You're getting ready to leave?' Another loud crack sounded and Stasy shook her head.

'Yes. We've been cleared to leave. I heard you managed to get my car back to the hospital after I left last night.'

'That's right. I headed back to the accident site and then drove your car to the hospital.'

'Thanks.'

'That's what girlfriends do.'

Justin was silent for a moment. 'Did you just say girlfriend?'

'Yes. That's what I am, right?'

'Oh, honey, you're much more than that but I'm just surprised to hear you say it out loud. I know you've been a little…hesitant.'

'Well, it's done.' Another crack came. 'Gee, there's a lot of thunder around. I hope the weather doesn't get worse as you get closer to home.'

'Home. I like the way that word sounds.'

'Me, too.' She paused. 'Call me when you're down safely. With this storm hanging overhead, I want to know you're safe.'

'Quite protective, aren't you?'

'Of mine? Yes. Get used to it.'

Again she could hear the smile in his voice. 'I intend to.'

He rang Stasy an hour later.

'Justin?'

'Yes.'

'Oh, thank goodness you're down.'

'Why?'

'The thunder. It's been getting worse.'

A prickle of apprehension washed over him. 'What thunder? It's raining, to be sure, but there's no thunder.'

'Sure there is. It's been happening all

morning. No lightning, thank goodness, but plenty of thunder. Where are you?'

'I've just left the hospital and I'm on my way to your place.'

A moment later, when the next loud crack came, Stasy almost dropped the phone. 'Surely you had to hear that?'

'More thunder?'

'You didn't hear it? You can't be *that* far away.'

'I'm not. It must be right over your house.'

'But there's no lightning. So strange.'

'Are you sure it's thunder?'

'What else could it be?'

'The kids are still with my parents, right?'

'Yes. According to your mother we're to have some time alone and then go over for lunch.'

'Sounds like a plan.' Justin chuckled and waited for Stasy to say something but she didn't. 'Stasy?' No reply. 'Stasy,' he said loudly. 'Anastasia?' It was then he realised the line had gone dead. He quickly redialled her number but couldn't get through. His heart started to pound wildly, his mind working even faster. What had happened? What was wrong?

The windscreen wipers were at full, swishing back and forth across the windscreen almost in a frenzy. The rain just wasn't letting up. The drops were big and heavy, the roads had puddles on either side. He was thankful he knew the road so well now as he increased his speed, desperate to get to Stasy's house to make sure she was all right. Nothing could happen to her. Not now.

He slowed the vehicle as he drew nearer to her property, his panic abating a little as the front of Stasy's house came in to view. Everything looked fine. Perhaps she'd tripped over the phone cord and pulled it out of the wall or something like that. Relaxing for a moment, he put his indicator on to turn into her driveway then slammed on the brakes.

There *was* no driveway. In its place was a hole in the ground.

Justin's chest tightened painfully as his apprehension and fear shot to boiling point. What on earth had happened? Quickly reversing, he parked the car on the opposite side of the road, switched on the hazard lights because of the dark clouds still gathering above, took a torch from the glove-box, then headed out to take a closer look at what had happened. Half of Stasy's house had disappeared. One of the trees out of the front yard was gone, too. Just gone!

Panic gripped him as he fumbled for his cellphone, dialling emergency services as he ran through the muddy ground, jumping the fence as he told the operator what he was seeing and where he was.

'I'll need ambulance, fire brigade and the police, too. Have the hospital on standby for retrieval if necessary.' With that, he snapped his phone shut and hooked it to his belt. Carefully navigating his way around the house, he managed to crawl in, calling for Stasy, but silence prevailed.

'No. No. She has to be all right. I've lost one woman I love and I'm not losing another.' Determination, if nothing else, was his best friend at the moment and he called her name again. As he ventured further into the house, he shook his head at what he saw. There was a yawning chasm right where her lounge room and kitchen should be. The torrential rain the city had experienced over the past few months had eroded and weakened the limestone beneath Stasy's house and as the district was riddled with little underground caves, the weight of the sodden ground and the house had been enough to collapse the roof of a cave under the property.

He directed the torch's light into the chasm and judged it to be about ten metres deep. The timbers were cracked, bits of masonry and glass shards were everywhere. Stasy's photographs, her books, her knick-knacks, DVDs were littered all over the place. Justin made his way carefully down a toppled tree, stopping every now and then to shine the beam of light around the place, wishing for one of the searchlights that had been at the accident site the night before.

'Stasy?' he called, but received no reply. When he was finally down on the ground, he picked his way to the kitchen, astonished at how the house had broken. It was as though someone had snapped it off and although it was at an angle, he was able to navigate the area quite well. Was she in the kitchen? He tried to think back to their phone conversation but couldn't remember.

As he rounded the corner into the kitchen, he saw her hand sticking out beneath bits of debris. 'Stasy!' Rushing to her side, Justin carefully picked the pieces of rubble from her face and then smoothed her hair back, checking her pulse. 'Stasy? Can you hear me?'

'Justin?' Her voice was weak but he heard it, heard the way she said his name.

'It's me, honey. I'm here. It's me.'

She coughed and he shifted more bits and pieces off her. Justin moved so he could get closer to her, needing to hold her but knowing he couldn't. She might have all sorts of injuries and he wasn't about to make things worse by losing his head and not following basic accident protocol. 'Oh, Stasy. I thought I'd lost you. I mean, I know it's ridiculous now that I've found you and that you're OK but I can't lose you. I just can't. I lost Rose and it nearly killed me. I can't lose you, too.'

With that he bent and kissed her face as tenderly and as carefully as though she were the most precious thing in the world. 'Does it hurt anywhere? Tell me, honey. Let me help you.'

Stasy tried to shift a little but Justin stopped her. 'Just wait. Help is on the way. Where does it hurt?'

'I can't tell but I can breathe, I can move my legs.'

'Good. That's good news.' He brushed his hand across her cheek. 'Oh my love. Don't you ever scare me like that again.'

She smiled. 'I'll try not to. I'll be all right. You're here now so I know I'll be fine.'

'You'd better believe it.' Justin shook his head. 'I thought…' He stopped. 'My mind went into overdrive when I thought I'd lost you just now.' He gently stroked her grimy face. 'I never want to part from you, Stasy Roberts. *Never*. You are my heart, and I can't imagine my life without you in it.'

Stasy gazed up at him. 'Is this your way of proposing?' she murmured weakly. She had listened to him, had watched the expressions on his face and seen so much. If she'd had any reservations about a future with him, they were completely gone now. He'd come and found her when she'd needed him most. He'd searched her out and had moved heaven and earth to get to her. Now he was telling her how much he loved her…*really* loved her…and she knew in that one split second that all her doubts had been washed away.

'I guess it is and I'm apparently doing a bad

job of it,' he said on a laugh. 'Well?' he asked when she didn't immediately reply.

She smiled. 'Oh. Sorry. I guess I'm doing a bad job of accepting.'

'Who cares? So long as we understand each other.'

'Very clearly. Come closer and I'll show you how clearly.'

He kissed her, very gently. Stasy knew she'd never get tired of Justin's kisses and she wanted heaps of them every day for the rest of her life.

Justin had been able to give the rescue crews clear and concise directions on where to find them, and it wasn't long before they came. Soon Stasy had been lifted out and was secured in the ambulance.

'The kids? Skye!' she said to Justin.

'We'll get you settled at the hospital, then I'll give Mum and Skye a call. There's no need to worry them unnecessarily.'

'True. And did you check on the animals?'

Justin smiled and stroked her hair. 'Yes, they were all out of harm's way. We'll have them all taken over to Mum's, so don't worry.'

At the hospital, Gene immediately took over Stasy's care. 'The left wrist is definitely broken,' he reported, looking at Stasy's X-rays. 'But nothing a cast won't fix.'

'Hold it up so I can see,' Stasy said.

'Now, now. You're the patient,' Justin remarked. 'Not the doctor.' Still, he held the radiograph up so she could see.

'Looks clean.'

'You've been very lucky, Stasy.' Gene packed up the X-rays. 'I'll get the bandages ready and then you can choose what colour cast you want on your arm.' He left them alone and Stasy closed her eyes for a moment.

'Tired?'

'Mmm.' She sighed and smiled at him. 'You rescued me.'

Justin returned her smile. 'I did, didn't I? I guess that makes me quite the hero.'

'Oh, yes. You were very heroic.'

'You think so?'

'I do.'

Justin couldn't believe how he felt when she looked at him the way she was. 'You know you're special to me.'

'I did sort of get that gist before when you said you loved me.'

'Really? Well, that's good…' he gazed deeply into her eyes '…because it's true.' He pressed his lips to hers, revelling in her touch, in the way they seemed to meld so perfectly together.

'Dad?' came a small voice from the doorway.

'Mum?' Two others chimed in.

Justin lifted his head, looking briefly at his darling Stasy before beckoning the children closer. They all came over and she reassured them, giving them each a hug and kiss.

'Are you really OK?' Tim wanted to know.

'I will be. I have a broken wrist and some bruised ribs but other than that, I'm fine.' Stasy saw Katherine and Herb in the doorway and asked them over. 'Actually,' she said, 'it's good that you're all here.' She looked to Justin and he came to stand by her, holding her unbroken hand. 'We have some news.'

'Oh!' Katherine clasped her hands together in excited anticipation.

'What? What is it?' Chelsea asked.

'Your mum and I,' Justin said, 'are going to get married!'

Katherine clapped her hands together and Herb came over to give his son a hearty pat on the back before leaning down to kiss Stasy. 'You're perfect for him,' he whispered.

'Thank you.'

'You're going to get *married*!' Chelsea's eyes were wide with shock.

'Is that all right?' Stasy asked, glancing at Justin with concern. 'I mean, it's not going to be straight away. The three of you need to get used to the idea first so we can take our time and—'

'Oh, my gosh!' Chelsea's squeal was so loud

Stasy grimaced. 'Mum! Hurry up and get better. We have to go shopping.'

Mike and Tim rolled their eyes. 'Girls,' they both said then, as though the truth of the matter hit them, they looked at each other. 'We'll be brothers!' They gave each other a high five.

Skye appeared in the doorway. 'Stasy! Are you all right? What happened?' She squeezed in to the room and went to her sister's side.

'Mum and Justin are getting married,' Chelsea announced.

'What?' Skye looked from one to the other. 'Honestly. I take one night off and the world seems to go crazy.'

Justin laughed.

'Where are we going to live?' Tim asked. 'From what Justin said, our house is totalled.'

'Well, I've been thinking on that all ready,' Justin replied. 'There's a house in the next street which is close to the hospital, close to the school, one block over from Mum and Dad, has five bedrooms, has a huge back yard and… guess what? It's up for sale.'

'We get a new house?' Mike was bug-eyed.

'This is so awesome,' Tim agreed.

'All right,' Gene said from outside the room. 'This place is far too crowded and I need to put a cast on your mum's arm,' he told all three kids.

'We'll go to the cafeteria,' Katherine said. 'Who wants ice cream?'

'Ice cream in the middle of winter,' Skye said, nodding. 'Lead the way.'

A moment later the cubicle was emptied of their family and Gene applied the cast. 'Now rest,' he ordered, and pointed to Justin. 'And I'm relying on you, Professor, to ensure she does.'

'You can count on me.'

When they were finally alone, Stasy smiled up at him. 'Well, that went well.'

'It did.' He sat on the bed beside her and placed his arm around her shoulders. 'What are we going to do with them?' he asked with love and happiness in his eyes.

'I'm not sure but I can't wait to find out!'

EPILOGUE

'You look beautiful, sis.' Skye held Stasy's hands and stepped back to look at her. The wedding dress was of ivory satin and came to mid-calf, the skirt full, the bodice fitted and strapless.

'It's true, Mum,' Chelsea agreed, still twirling the skirt of her bridesmaid's dress. She'd been unable to stop from the moment she'd put it on.

'Justin is a lucky man.'

'Oh, I think Stasy's just as lucky to be getting my son for a husband,' Katherine said as she came over to kiss the bride. They were all standing beneath a marquee which had been erected to shade the bride from the warm December sun. Both Justin and Stasy had wanted to wait a few months, first of all so the children were used to the idea of being together as a family but also because Stasy had refused to get married with a purple cast on her arm.

Stasy hugged Katherine close. 'I can't believe my life has turned out this way. Not only am I gaining a fantastic husband in Justin but I get Mike as my son and you two as well.' She held out her hand to Herb as she spoke and he crossed to her side. 'Even after Skye and I lost our parents, you were both there and now… you'll be family in every sense of the word.' Stasy sniffed but her smile was bright.

'Now, now,' Katherine said, sniffing as well. 'You don't want to ruin your make-up, especially when we only have a few more minutes.'

Stasy took a deep breath and looked with love at those around her. The boys were waiting for them, waiting for them all to walk down the centre aisle of Umpherson's sink hole. The day was warm but not a scorcher and the garden below them was filled with an abundance of flowers in a range of colours.

As the wedding march began, all Stasy's earlier nerves fled. She would soon be standing by Justin's side and with him there beside her for the rest of her life, she knew she could cope with anything that came their way.

'Ready?' Herb asked, and crooked his arm at her.

'Ready.'

'I still say I'm far too old to be the matron of honour,' Katherine grumbled good-naturedly, and Stasy recalled how she'd managed to over come the other woman's protests.

'I go first, don't I?' Chelsea asked and Stasy bent down to kiss her beautiful daughter.

'Yes, you do, darling. Just as we rehearsed.'

'OK.' Chelsea took her position at the top of the steps that led down into the sink hole. Skye would follow her, then Katherine and finally Herb and Stasy. Thankfully, none of them tripped on the steps, as they'd often joked about, and soon she was walking towards Justin. She was glad she'd decided against a veil because as soon as she met the glorious brown of his rich, deep eyes, she was just as hypnotised as she'd been the first time she'd met him.

Mike stood proudly beside his father as the official best man and Tim stood beside his soon-to-be brother as groomsman. When Herb handed Stasy over to Justin, an upwelling of love overcame her and she thought she might burst in to tears right there and then but the warmth of Justin's hand on hers steadied her— as she knew it always would.

'Dearly beloved,' the minister began. 'We are gathered here—'

'Just a moment,' Justin said softly, stopping him. A collective gasp could be heard from everyone around them but Stasy knew there was nothing wrong. She *knew* that look in Justin's eyes, she *knew* what it meant because she *knew* him so very well. Without another word, he leaned forward and pressed his lips to hers in the most glorious welcoming kiss she'd ever experienced. The friends who had come to see them unite as husband and wife cheered and clapped. The minister cleared his throat.

'I haven't got to that part yet,' he whispered.

Justin pulled back, smiled brightly at his blushing bride, and then nodded. 'Then get to it quickly because I am one impatient man.'

Thankfully, the rest of the ceremony proceeded without a hitch and soon the minister got to 'that part' after declaring them husband and wife.

'For ever,' Stasy said as she looked at the plain gold band on her finger, the one that had no beginning and no end but went on for ever…like Justin's love.

'For ever,' he replied, and held her close.

MEDICAL™

Large Print

Titles for the next six months...

December

SINGLE DAD SEEKS A WIFE	Melanie Milburne
HER FOUR-YEAR BABY SECRET	Alison Roberts
COUNTRY DOCTOR, SPRING BRIDE	Abigail Gordon
MARRYING THE RUNAWAY BRIDE	Jennifer Taylor
THE MIDWIFE'S BABY	Fiona McArthur
THE FATHERHOOD MIRACLE	Margaret Barker

January

VIRGIN MIDWIFE, PLAYBOY DOCTOR	Margaret McDonagh
THE REBEL DOCTOR'S BRIDE	Sarah Morgan
THE SURGEON'S SECRET BABY WISH	Laura Iding
PROPOSING TO THE CHILDREN'S DOCTOR	Joanna Neil
EMERGENCY: WIFE NEEDED	Emily Forbes
ITALIAN DOCTOR, FULL-TIME FATHER	Dianne Drake

February

THEIR MIRACLE BABY	Caroline Anderson
THE CHILDREN'S DOCTOR AND THE SINGLE MUM	Lilian Darcy
THE SPANISH DOCTOR'S LOVE-CHILD	Kate Hardy
PREGNANT NURSE, NEW-FOUND FAMILY	Lynne Marshall
HER VERY SPECIAL BOSS	Anne Fraser
THE GP'S MARRIAGE WISH	Judy Campbell

MILLS & BOON
Pure reading pleasure™

MEDICAL™

Large Print

March

SHEIKH SURGEON CLAIMS HIS BRIDE Josie Metcalfe
A PROPOSAL WORTH WAITING FOR   Lilian Darcy
A DOCTOR, A NURSE: A LITTLE MIRACLE Carol Marinelli
TOP-NOTCH SURGEON, PREGNANT NURSE Amy Andrews
A MOTHER FOR HIS SON   Gill Sanderson
THE PLAYBOY DOCTOR'S MARRIAGE   Fiona Lowe
PROPOSAL

April

A BABY FOR EVE   Maggie Kingsley
MARRYING THE MILLIONAIRE DOCTOR   Alison Roberts
HIS VERY SPECIAL BRIDE   Joanna Neil
CITY SURGEON, OUTBACK BRIDE   Lucy Clark
A BOSS BEYOND COMPARE   Dianne Drake
THE EMERGENCY DOCTOR'S   Molly Evans
CHOSEN WIFE

May

DR DEVEREUX'S PROPOSAL   Margaret McDonagh
CHILDREN'S DOCTOR,   Meredith Webber
MEANT-TO-BE WIFE
ITALIAN DOCTOR, SLEIGH-BELL BRIDE Sarah Morgan
CHRISTMAS AT WILLOWMERE   Abigail Gordon
DR ROMANO'S CHRISTMAS BABY   Amy Andrews
THE DESERT SURGEON'S SECRET SON   Olivia Gates

⊚™MILLS & BOON®
Pure reading pleasure™   1108 LP 2P P2 Medical